GILDED LIES

The Devil's Bargain Series

SARA MCCLAFLIN

First Edition

ASIN: B0DYB8XNJ3

ISBN (trade): 979-8-9914135-8-9

Book Cover by Pia

Editing: Brandy Gibson

Social Media: Tawny Gratto

PA: Ashley Sullivan

Marketing & PR: Wildfire Marketing Solutions

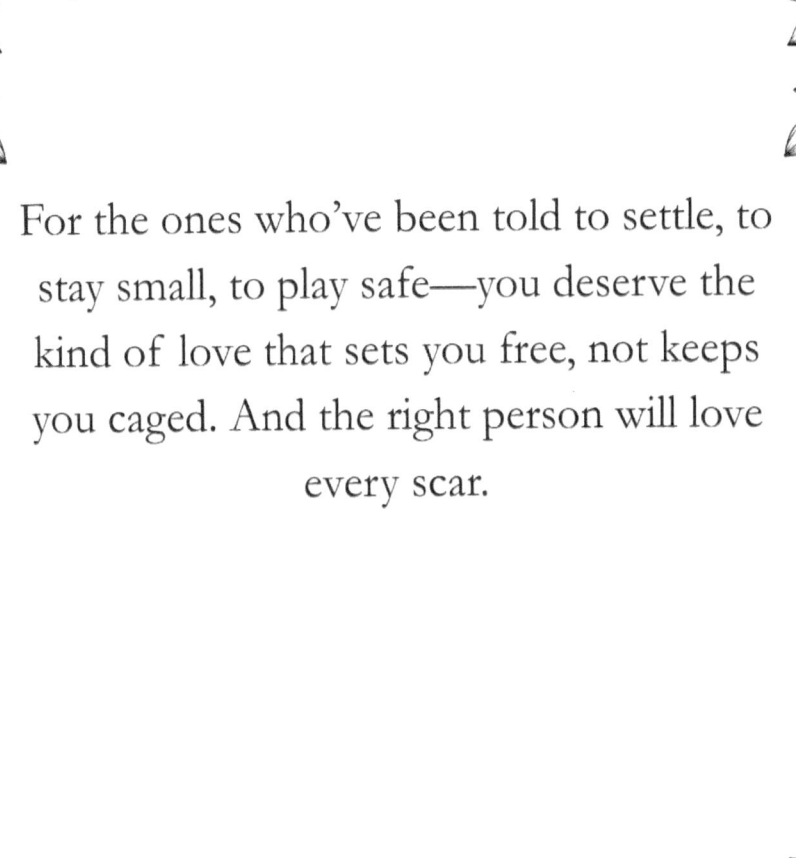

For the ones who've been told to settle, to stay small, to play safe—you deserve the kind of love that sets you free, not keeps you caged. And the right person will love every scar.

Author Note

When I started writing Bella's story, I thought I knew the path she'd take—turns out she had other ideas. What began as a story about second chances quickly became a journey about power, trust, and the courage it takes to let someone in all the way.

She eclipses everything I thought she could be, and Owen became the knight in shining armor I didn't know she needed.

This book let me explore the beauty and brutality of love when it's forged in fire, and the found family that makes surviving Hell (literal or otherwise) not just possible, but worth it.

If you made it this far, thank you for loving these characters through all their flaws and victories. I'm so glad you're here.

And as for what's next? Let's just say...the story isn't over yet.

Content Warning

This book contains mature content and situations intended for adult readers (18+). Some of the events, conflicts, or character backstories may touch on sensitive topics.

Reader discretion is strongly advised.

If you'd like to see a detailed list of possible triggers and content notes before you begin, I've prepared one for you on my website: https://www.authorsaramcclaflin.com/gilded-lies

Contents

The Demon's Oath

The Demon's Oath

A Sacred Vow of Binding and Judgment

By the Depths of the Abyss, by the Shadows That Watch, by the Chains of Fate that no force may sever–

Let it be written. Let it be known. Let it be sealed.

I, **Owen Duvain**, of my own will and without coercion, do stand before the Unseen Council and swear this Oath, binding my existence to the Eternal Laws of Bargains, Punishments, and the Seven Sins.

I take upon myself the mantle of **Deal Maker and Deliverer of Judgment.**

I wield not the sword, but the contract, for a promise is sharper than any blade.

I wield not chains, but consequence, for a choice freely made is a fate unchangeable.

I wield not force, but inevitability, for what is agreed shall come to pass, no matter the pleading.

I walk among mortals not as a savior, but as a test–**to tempt, to offer, and to take.**

Thus, before the **Shrouded Thrones and the Abyssal Hosts**, I inscribe my vow into the **Book of Binding**, knowing that once my name is burned into these pages, my path is set.

THE LAWS OF THE OATH

I. The Deal is the Beginning.

To speak is to shape. To offer is to bind. Once my words seal a deal, there shall be no undoing, no regret, no escape.

II. The Bargain Holds Weight.

What is given shall not be returned. What is promised shall not be denied. No mortal, angel, or demon shall unravel the contract once it is set.

III. The Cost Shall Match the Desire.

Each soul shall be measured, and its burden weighed. The greater the sin, the greater the consequence. No deal shall be granted without its proper price.

IV. The Collector Does Not Pity.

I shall not sway, nor shall I falter. I shall take what is owed in its due time. No tears, no pleas, no prayers shall alter fate.

V. The Soulmate is Fate, But Duty is Eternal.

If I should find the one who bears my mark, the soul bound to mine by fate, I shall not deny them, for fate cannot be rewritten. To love is not a sin, but to forsake my duty for love is unforgivable.

Though my soul may recognize its other half, my purpose remains unshaken. I shall not waver, nor shall I allow this bond to weaken the will I have sworn to uphold.

If I place my soulmate above my duty, if I let them turn me from my path, then let my name be burned from the Abyss, my power stripped, and my soul cast into the void, lost to both fate and eternity.

VI. The Unseen Council Holds the Final Word.

Though their presence is unknown, their law is absolute. No punishment shall be given beyond what is agreed, and no deal shall be struck that defies the Balance.

VII. The Reckoning Shall Always Come.

No bargain shall go uncollected. No debtor shall go unpunished. In pain or in ruin, in torment or in nothingness—the price shall be paid.

SO IT IS WRITTEN.

SO IT IS SEALED.

SO IT SHALL BE.

SIGNED IN BLOOD AND HELLFIRE BEFORE THE UN-SEEN COUNCIL

Owen Duvain

Signed in Blood, Marked by the Shadows, Sealed in Fire

Prologue
Owen

A nother day, another deal.

I think that's the saying. It's my saying, anyway.

Truthfully, I like mortals. Not for their charm–don't be ridiculous–but for how fast they crumble. A little fame, a little fortune, and suddenly they're on their knees, begging to sign.

Souls are currency. And I like collecting.

Unlike most of my family, I enjoy leaving the underworld. Except for Seth. That idiot practically has a punch card for his mortal affairs.

Julian found his soulmate–good for him, great for the rest of us. It keeps Mother and Selene distracted with their wedding plans, which leaves them with less time to crawl up my spine.

Caleb and Adrian only leave when the air gets too still. They like the fallout, not the fire. Lucas waits, always two moves ahead—he's never surprised, just disappointed. And Damian doesn't move unless it's going to make an impact on more than just the person making the bargain.

We're all incredibly different. But we're blood. Demon blood.

I like getting out, seeing the others, and taking in the new souls. My morning walks through the marketplace are one of my favorite parts of my daily routine.

The Veil Marketplace is in the center of Hell, similar to a city center on Earth. There are stalls and sellers of all kinds of goods. From soul jewelry to truth blades, anything and everything one could think of is here.

It's also the epicenter of power in our realm. Other than where the Infernal Council convenes, of course.

I can hear the calls stronger here.

"Ah here comes one now," I chuckle to myself.

I'm being summoned, but not by name. This is not someone who knows me. With a snort, I roll my eyes, I can practically smell the desperation from here.

I call to the ones who walk between shadow and flame. Let one who would bargain step forth.

I hear it—so it's mine. Let the games begin.

I arrived at a man's house, the smell gives it away, expensive cologne. This is going to be a good exchange. I love rich people, they think they can escape anything, it makes this process much more fun.

A bit of white chalk on the floor catches my eyes, a sigil is drawn on the ground. The laugh that bursts from my mouth is completely out of my control. Julian warned me that rich people have started to try and trap us.

I've just never seen one before.

"What are you laughing at?" An angry voice snaps from the darkness.

"At you thinking you can contain me," I say, amusement leaking through my voice.

I step out of the trap and hear a gasp. With a flick of my hand, the light switch across the room lifts, illuminating the space.

"That's better," I say.

"Holy shit," another voice, male, says. "I can't believe this worked." He sounds...giddy? Weird.

"Why was I summoned?" I ask, getting to the chase, these men are boring me already. I already know the answer, but it's fun to watch them squirm.

"To make a deal," the older man says.

"And you are?"

"I'm Ellison Creed and this is my son Sterling," he says, like I should know based on their names.

"I didn't ask for your names," I start, earning myself a glare from them. "I asked *who* you are."

"I'm the CEO of Creed Core Development and a Real Estate Developer," the young one says. "My dad is the mayor."

I tilt my head, just enough to be condescending. "You summoned a soul collector. You must want something you can't take."

I don't actually care who these people are.. But how they introduce themselves tells me how desperate they are to matter.

Sterling puffs up. Amateur move. I stop myself from rolling my eyes outright.

Ellison lifts a hand, silencing his son before he can speak. He smooths his voice like he's on the campaign trail and doing backroom deals.

"My son wants the future," he says simply. "The lights. The leverage. A seat at the table when the world reshapes itself." *Are these guys conspiracy theorists or just dramatic?*

Sterling doesn't speak–he doesn't need to. He radiates entitlement.

Ellison continues, slower now. "We already control this city. But legacy?" He looks at Owen. "That takes more."

"You've already risked your souls just calling me here," I say. "So ask. What are you willing to give up to win?"

"We spoke to Cassius Arden," Sterling says. "Before he disappeared."

Just the name has fire burning through my body. I don't react, but something flashes in my eyes for just a second.

Ellison flinches. His breath stutters. He steps back, like instinct tells him what his mind won't admit.

"He told us that you don't have to sell a soul. That you can switch gifts and sell someone else's," Sterling says, completely missing what has struck a deep, cold fear in his father's heart—or whatever he has in that hollow space in his chest.

"You aren't afraid or desperate," I say, turning to him.

"No," he starts. "I know a good deal when I see one."

"Fine. What do you want to trade?"

"I want to trade my idiot sister's soul," he says, showing me a photograph.

Something about her feels familiar. I can't put my finger on it. Probably nothing. "Why her?"

Sterling shrugs. Too casual. "She wants to turn our brand into a fucking charity. It's pathetic," he says, like it's the worst offense imaginable.

So, she's not awful, just inconvenient. What's worse, *she makes him look weak. And that? Unforgivable.*

I glance at Ellison, waiting for him to object. Of course he doesn't. The rot doesn't fall far from the tree.

"Okay," I say, getting right in their faces. "Let's make a deal shall we."

I step back and will a contract to appear in my hands. I love this moment. It gives me the warm and fuzzies inside.

Watching mortals think they're getting everything they want never gets old.

"The terms are simple," I say, staring at the contract. "Your sister's soul will be added to my collection–eventually. Any good fortune will be switched to you."

I turn the page with a flick of my fingers. "You'll get the gift slowly."

"What?!" Sterling exclaims. "I want it now!"

"There is no editing this," I snap. "Ink your names in blood, gentlemen. Or walk away and waste all our time."

They both give in quickly, cutting themselves and signing their name in their own blood.

"Good," I say, letting the contract disappear. It's now in the hands of the archivists to keep an eye on. "Your deal is complete."

I leave before they can say anything else. My part's done—until it's time to collect.

I don't bother mentioning their souls are bound now. If they've dealt with Cassius, they already know.

And they didn't ask, so it's not my problem.

Ophelia gave Cassius and Melanie their punishment, but I feel like I need to tell them about Cassius opening his mouth. Maybe even give him a little visit.

I'll start with Julian and Ophelia. I used to just appear in his living room. But now that he's with his soulmate–I think it's best if I knock. I don't want to see things I shouldn't.

"Hey," Julian says, answering the door, thankfully fully clothed. "You look serious."

"Owen!" Ophelia exclaims. "What's wrong? Are you okay? Let him in, Julian."

"I was just about to, Little Artist," he says, smiling down at her.

"You guys are gross," I say, pretending to dry heave.

"Yeah yeah. Wait until you find yours," Julian quips back.

"Your parents are here with your aunt and uncle," Ophelia says, as we walk in.

Their living room is covered with Union materials of all kinds—a stack of black wax sealed papers, a banner with a thorned crest, and a pile of brass tokens that look like they belong in a vault, not on a coffee table.

"Owen," my mother, Liora, says. "What are you doing here?"

"Sorry to ruin the mood, but we need to talk about Cassius," I say.

"Cassius?" Ophelia asks, brows drawn as she whips her attention to me. "Why?"

"Your father opened his mouth, Ophelia," I start. "I just signed a deal with two people tried to trap me."

"So?" Julian says. "Mortals have been doing that for years, even though it is rare, it's not unheard of."

"They said that *he* told them that they could sell another soul and get what they want," I say.

"Damn that dude was cocky. Did he really think he'd be able to get away with everything?" Julian says.

Ophelia doesn't flinch. "He absolutely did, you've met him. We're going to see him."

The chamber reeks of pain.

Old blood, old sins, old air that's never seen daylight. The walls drip with it—regret carved into stone, bones ground into mortar.

Cassius' screams reach our ears before we enter.

We step through the threshold one by one. Liora first. Evander and Theron like shadows behind her. Selene doesn't blink. Julian doesn't speak.

I don't stop walking.

Cassius is already half-flayed, strung up like a ruined marionette. There are hooks in his wrists, and chains biting through his spine. His skin is peeled back in ribbons that drip like wax.

When Ophelia walks in the gravity changes. The room bends around her. The power of hell makes itself known through her anger. I don't believe in omens, but if I did? She'd be one.

She moves straight to him, boots splashing through blood like it's water, eyes locked on his ruined face.

Cassius tries to laugh, but it comes out more as a gurgle of teeth and blood.

She raises one hand—and with a flick of her wrist, she slices open the soft part of his stomach. Just enough to remind him there's worse to come.

He screams again.

Julian watches her like she's art in motion.

I watch the blood run toward my boot and wonder how much of this was predictable.

Cassius is laughing again—bloody and broken as it is.

"Creed and his son?" I ask, stepping forward.

He lifts his head, or tries to. One eye glares through blood. "Ah. So they made a deal..." He grins, wide and red. "This should be fun."

Ophelia's blade twitches. She's not done.

But I speak first, trying to calm her down. "Let him scream another day."

"Fine," she says. She slices a thin line down his cheek. He screams. Again. She drops the blade and laughs at him as she stands beside Julian.

Julian exhales like a man who just remembered how.

I watch the blood drip. And wonder—how much worse this will get before we're done pretending to be civilized.

Chapter One
Arabella

I wake up disoriented, the kind of groggy that doesn't feel like sleep but like I blacked out. My head's heavy, my mouth dry, and something inside me feels off-kilter.

The air's strange. It's still, not wrong exactly, but off in a way I can't name. It presses at the edges of the apartment like it's waiting for me to notice something.

My studio is barely more than a box. Tucked into the top floor of the Hearthlight Center, it's got uneven walls, a stubborn radiator, and one window that sticks when it rains. The bigger apartments went to families who needed space. I took the smallest one and made it work.

Rhys asked me to move into his place after we got married, but I hated that cold, industrial loft. Here, I'm a hallway away from Hearthlight if an emergency hits, and I like my space the way it is.

When Tom retired, I didn't just take over as director. He left Hearthlight to me—literally. Signed over the land and the building. Said I fought for this place, so I should be the one to protect it.

So now it's mine. All of it. The walls, the programs, the lives inside them. The debt.

And this morning, something feels *wrong*.

Not in the building. In me.

There's a pressure in my chest. A slow, hot throb that gets worse the more I try to ignore it. At first, I think it's anxiety. Maybe I'm still wound up from the wedding. From Ophelia glowing and Rhys hovering and all that magic in the air, I didn't know how to breathe.

But then the burning starts.

I wince and sit up too fast, my head spinning. The bedsheet sticks to the sweat at the base of my neck. My shirt's soaked through, clinging to skin that feels scorched from the inside out. There's panic setting in as I try to pant through the pain. Then I look down. It wasn't a dream.

It's right there. It looks almost identical to my sister's.

The Mark of Duvain.

My heart drops.

It's not supposed to be me. I'm married. This isn't how it's supposed to happen.

But it's there. Etched into my skin like it's always been there. Like it's waiting.

"Shit," I whisper. My voice is dry. My whole body feels hijacked.

The last thing I remember is the wedding. Ophelia's eyes, Rhys's hand in mine, the way the world seemed to tilt around the edges. Next, pain like something inside me was tearing loose and taking pieces with it.

I reach up to touch the mark again, but the room creaks.

Not from the heater. From footsteps.

Someone's here.

My heart climbs into my throat, I'm about to scream.

"You're awake," Owen says, stepping through the doorway like he's been here all night.

He looks... calm. Too calm for someone who just claimed my soul. His coat's still on, collar turned up. He doesn't move closer, he just stands there, watching me from beneath lashes too dark and eyes too knowing.

"How long have you been here?" My voice is hoarse. I can still feel the rawness in my throat from screaming in pain.

"Since I carried you out of the party."

I clutch the blanket tighter. My fingers tremble. "You shouldn't be here."

"Probably not," he says, gaze flicking to the mark at my collarbone. "But neither should that."

I follow his eyes. The mark glows faintly beneath my skin—proof that whatever tether snapped into place that night hasn't faded. If anything, it's stronger.

"What does it mean?" I ask, even though I already know. The bond. The fate. The end of everything I thought I had. Of everything I told myself I wanted.

"It means you were never his to begin with," he says.

"I married him," I say, like it matters.

"I know."

"I made vows."

"And fate didn't care." Which was funny, since my sister was supposed to be in charge of it.

I go still. My fingers twitch at the edge of the blanket. I feel... exposed. But not in the way I thought I would. Not embarrassed or ashamed.

Just seen. And I hate that it's *him* seeing me.

I don't have time to say anything else. Not like I would know what to say anyway. Because while my brain stutters, the front door swings open.

Rhys steps inside, his tie's loose, sleeves rolled to the elbow.

"Oh," he says, eyes locking on Owen and narrowing. "Of course. You've got a lot of nerve showing up here."

"I carried her out of a room full of demons," Owen replies, cool and unmoved. "She nearly collapsed."

"She's my wife," Rhys growls, stepping closer. "Mine. I got there first. Whatever this is—whatever you think it is—it's not real."

Owen doesn't blink. Doesn't say a thing, just lets him rant.

"She made vows to me," Rhys goes on, voice rising. "You think you can just swoop in and take what isn't yours?"

"I'm not a prize," I snap, turning toward him. "Don't talk about me like I'm something you get to win."

Rhys stiffens. "Bella, come on. This isn't you. You're upset. He's confusing you."

"I'm not confused," I say, jaw tight. "I'm angry."

"You're poisoning her," Rhys spits, eyes cutting back to Owen.

"I'm telling her the truth," Owen says. His jaw ticks, but he doesn't move. His eyes flick to mine, asking for something I'm not sure I can give.

"I need to talk to him," I say quietly.

Owen nods once. "If you need me,"

"I'll find you," I say, cutting him off.

He looks at Rhys like he wants to say something else. Maybe a warning. Maybe a promise. But instead, he turns and walks out without another word.

The door clicks shut. And suddenly it's just me and Rhys.

"Well?" I ask, arms crossed.

"I hate the way he looks at you," he mutters.

"You don't get to act territorial now just because fate stepped in," I say, stepping forward.

"I'm your husband. It's my job to protect you," Rhys shouts, throwing his hands in the air like that settles it.

I wince. Not because he is loud, but because of the absurdity.

"I get that. I do," I say, trying to get him to quiet down. "I get that you want to fix this. I get that you think you've earned something."

"But?" His voice cracks. He's barely hanging on.

"But this mark is changing things, Rhys. You and I both know that." I hold his gaze. "It's not just something I can turn off."

"Nothing is changing for me," he spits, stepping forward. "I made vows, Bella. I stood there and meant them."

He might as well be stomping his feet at this point.

"Well, everything has changed for me," I say, trying to stay calm. "Ophelia got sick when she was separated from Julian. She nearly died. The bond doesn't just go away."

"And you're saying you believe that?" he sneers. "That magic and prophecy matter more than marriage, more than us?"

"I'm saying..." I breathe in through my nose. "I have to trust fate. And maybe there's another way through this—but it doesn't look like denial."

He's silent. Furious and still.

"Did you marry me," I ask softly, "because you loved me? Or because you thought I was safe?"

His jaw tightens. "That's not fair."

"No, Rhys. What's *not* fair is pretending this bond doesn't exist because it's inconvenient for *you*."

I step back, something cold settling in my bones.

"I didn't ask for any of this," I say. "But I'm not going to be punished for it, either."

He doesn't follow. He doesn't speak. He just watches me walk away—like I've become someone he doesn't understand.

And maybe I have.

Chapter Two
Owen

I leave Arabella's apartment and go straight to the Duvain thinking zone.

Ophelia built a garden that sits between our properties. A Hell garden, because of course she did. If there's a place for art, Ophelia's going to fill it.

We all thought it was ridiculous. Unnecessary. A vanity project made of flame-touched soil and drama.

And yet—one by one—we all end up here when we need to think.

I sit on the bench and look at everything around me.

It's not peaceful, exactly. The trees hum low with magic, leaves like molten glass swaying in air that doesn't move. The flowers bloom in deep, violent reds and bruised purples, their petals edged in something that looks suspiciously like ash. It's beauty designed to fit right into hell.

A pond cuts through the middle, dark as oil, lit from below by veins of silver light that don't reflect anything real.

It's all so Ophelia—dangerous and defiant and impossible not to look at.

I drag a hand through my hair and lean back. *What the hell is happening?* I don't just feel the mark on Bella. I feel *her*. Even now. A slow, hot ache that won't let up.

And Rhys? He doesn't just feel wrong. He *is* wrong. And if he thinks this is something he can still control...

He has no idea what kind of war he just walked into.

"You look lost," Ophelia says, her voice drifting across the stone path like smoke.

"Understatement of the millennium, Lia," I mutter, managing a half-chuckle.

I glance up. "You two always come in pairs now?"

"Only when the other is spiraling," Julian says mildly, taking his spot against a column.

Ophelia drops beside me on the bench. "You haven't gone back to her."

"She needs time," I say.

"And you're okay giving it?" she asks.

"No," I answer honestly. "I keep checking on her through the bond. It's killing me."

She smiles, not unkindly. "Then why aren't you there?"

"Because I want her to choose me. Not the bond. Not the ache. *Me.*"

"What did it feel like? When it hit?" Ophelia asks me.

I stare down at my hands. Hoping for a reason to not answer this. Not be this vulnerable with someone else.

"It didn't feel like I thought it would," I say. "Not like everyone warned. There wasn't any dread behind it. It felt... inevitable. Like she'd been mine for a thousand lifetimes and I'd just been waiting for her to remember."

Julian hums. "Soulmarks don't lie. They just don't explain themselves. Besides, you've been asking the wrong people about being marked."

"I'm Greed." I get up, throwing my hands in the air basically shouting at the universe. "I've built my whole life on wanting. Deals, power, leverage—I've taken everything I could get my hands on. But her? I don't want to take a damn thing. I just want to give. All of it. Everything I have."

"Why does it feel like love when you talk about her?" Ophelia's lips curve into a knowing smile.

"Because it is," I snap. "But not the kind people write songs about. Not flowers and candlelight and easy promises. It's deeper. Messier. I don't just want her happiness—I want to be the reason for it. I want her rage, her stubbornness, her worst days. I want the version of her no one else has the right to touch. The one she hides from everyone. And I want her to give it to me willingly."

"You think she can love the darkest parts of you," Julian says, watching me carefully.

"No," I reply. "I *know* she already does. She just hasn't realized it yet."

Ophelia's eyes soften. "She always loved too gently. Thought she had to be easy to love. Rhys took advantage of that."

"She wants what you two have," I say. "I want to give it to her. I want to take away very goddamn scar she carries."

Julian shifts. "So what's stopping you?"

I look out at the glowing thorns curling through her garden.

"I can't be the reason she doubts her own choices. She's not a possession. She's the one I didn't know I needed."

Ophelia scoffs. "Rhys treats her like she is one. Like love's a contract with fine print she wasn't smart enough to read."

Julian raises a brow, but doesn't argue. He's heard it all before.

"She's always wanted love to mean safety," Ophelia continues, eyes sharp. "He sold her that story. White picket fence. Good job. A family.

She clung to it because it was there and easy. But it was never love. Not real love anyway."

Julian cuts in, his voice thoughtful. "You think she regrets it?"

"No," Ophelia says. "But she's starting to see it for what it is. That will terrify her."

I say nothing, jaw tight. Because she's right.

"She wants what we have," Julian says after a pause, eyes soft on Ophelia. "That pull. That madness. That truth."

"Rhys doesn't have the capacity for it," Ophelia says, biting the words off. "He performs affection. Measures commitment in calendar invites and dinner reservations. But he doesn't *feel* it. Not in his bones. Not like we do."

The air shimmers once before splitting down the middle like reality decided to unzip itself. A woman steps through it like she's done it a thousand times before.

Her coat flares around her legs, braids threaded with silver cuffs catching the glow of the thornlight. Skin kissed by sun and shadow, sigils faint on her forearms. Her eyes—green and gold and impossible to pin down—take in everything at once. She smells like honey, old magic, and something sharp beneath. The air tilts around her. Not threatened. Just aware. Like the realm knows this is not a woman to underestimate.

Julian straightens instantly. "Who the hell—?"

Ophelia doesn't blink. "Della Sage."

"You *know* her?" I ask, already on my feet.

"We met," she says, glancing at Julian. "At Hex & Brews. Bella took me. She said Della had... unusual insights."

"Unusual?" Julian echoes.

"She reads the weave of things," Ophelia says. "And walks between planes like most of us walk across a street."

"Your timing's convenient," I say, voice low.

Della shrugs, a small knowing smile touching her lips. "I don't operate on your timelines. I go where I'm pulled. And tonight, the pull came straight through your lovely little murder garden."

Her eyes flick to me.

"You're burning hot," she says, nodding towards the horizon, voice cooling. "But she's the one lighting up every ward this side of the veil. And someone's already circling."

Della lifts one hand, fingers splayed. Gold and green sparks dance across her palm, flickering like fireflies caught in a storm.

"She's more than marked," she says, eyes glowing. "She's humming. Loud. Enough that every veil-walker, soul-broker, and cursed thing within fifty miles is sniffing the air."

She closes her fist, and the sparks vanish.

"I tried to stay out of it. Fate's a pushy bitch, but I've learned not to poke her unless I have to. But *he* started sniffing out stories that weren't his to tell."

Julian narrows his gaze. "Rhys?"

"Your garden-variety narcissist with a press badge," Della replies, rolling her eyes. "Investigative reporter, hungry for legacy. And the Creeds knew it. They dangled the bait—Bella, Hearthlight, the Duvain name—and told him to dig."

Julian tenses beside me, gold flashing behind his irises.

"He thought he was exposing corruption," Della continues, walking slowly, her boots clicking on the obsidian. "That Hearthlight was laundering something. That the Duvains were tied to the land. That Bella didn't deserve to own it. And when he couldn't find the dirt he wanted—he made it."

Ophelia's brows draw together. "How?"

"He started gaslighting her. Undermining her decisions. Telling her to quit. That she was in over her head." Della stops, turning toward Ophelia. "He was supposed to wear her down, not fall for her. But he did. Stupidly. Sloppily. And now the Creeds are furious."

"Because they were using him to get her to sell," I mutter, jaw tight. The words taste bitter.

Della nods, slow and sharp. "They promised him front-page legacy. Fame. The man who cracked open the supernatural elite. He thought Hearthlight was just the story—until she became the prize."

Julian exhales through his nose. "And now?"

"They're cutting their losses," Della replies, voice cooling. "Scrubbing the evidence. Bella is the last thread. She owns the land. The wards. The name. She makes the place untouchable and that makes her dangerous."

Ophelia folds her arms. "And Rhys?"

"Oh, he's furious," Della says, the corner of her mouth twitching. "Not just because he lost control of the story—but because you," she nods at me, "got marked."

My spine stiffens.

"He thinks everything should be his," she goes on. "The promotion, the credit, the girl. He was groomed for ownership, and now fate's laughing in his face."

Julian tilts his head. "So now he's spiraling."

"No," Della corrects. "He's plotting."

Her gaze snaps to mine. "Do you love her?"

I don't hesitate. "More than anything."

Della's smile is gleaming like a blade in moonlight. "You'd better be ready to fight for her. Because Rhys still thinks this is a game and he's not used to losing."

Chapter Three
Arabella

T his is all becoming too much. I haven't spoken to Rhys or Owen in weeks. I don't know who I actually want to see more.

Not to mention work is never ending. It's like there's an uptick of people in this city that need the help we provide.

Right when I thought I would get a moment to myself, my office door opens. Rhys walks in.

"We need to talk, Bells," he says. He looks exhausted. Like he hasn't slept in months.

"You could've called." I stand to walk right in front of him. I've had enough.

"Would you have answered?" He counters, crossing his arms.

"How could you know I wouldn't? You haven't tried." I place a hand on my hip. I'm sure I look like a child, but I've had enough. The last thing I can handle is him acting like the entitled man-child he can be when he doesn't get his way.

"Neither did you," he scoffs.

He does have a point. Maybe we've been avoiding each other. I wanted so much more from my marriage than this.

"Fine. What did you want to talk about?" I cross my arms, my voice tight.

"Us," Rhys says, like that should mean something.

"Okay. Talk," I reply, eyes narrowing.

"I've been thinking... maybe we could leave all this behind," he says, stepping closer.

"All what?" I ask, even though I already have an idea of what he means.

"The center. The city. The stress. You've been running yourself ragged. And now with everything that's happened—maybe it's a sign," he says, his tone too careful.

"A sign?" I echo, skeptical.

"We could go somewhere new. Start over. I've got a contact upstate, a real estate friend. There's a cottage. Secluded. Peaceful," he continues, his voice soft like he's trying to sell me a dream.

"You want me to quit Hearthlight?" I ask, disbelief creeping into my voice.

"I want you to be happy. And maybe... finally free of the pressure. No more crisis calls at midnight. No more burnouts. Just you and me. We could build something real," Rhys says, reaching for my hand, but I step back.

"I *am* building something real, Rhys. It's called community. Hearthlight matters," I say, my voice sharper than I intended.

"You don't owe that place your life, Bella. You've already given enough. Maybe it's time to choose *you*. To choose *us*," he says, frustration bleeding into the edges of his voice.

"So, selling it off is choosing me?" I ask, shifting my weight like I'm preparing for a fight.

"It's not like that," he says quickly.

"It sure as hell feels like that's exactly what you're saying, Rhys," I shoot back.

"I know you feel something's shifting. Between us. And I don't want to lose what we have just because things are complicated. I want to try, Bella. I want us to have a real shot," he says, stepping closer again like proximity can fix what's broken.

"You're asking me to walk away from the one thing I've built on my own," I say, voice low.

"I'm asking you to walk toward something better," he says, almost pleading.

I just stare at him.

"You mean with you," I say finally, trying to process the weight of what he's asking. "You want me to walk away from my work, my people, my purpose—so I can go play house in the woods with the man who's barely looked me in the eyes for weeks?"

"Don't twist it," Rhys says, jaw tightening. "This is about us, Bella. I'm trying to save what we have."

"By tearing down everything that makes me who I am?" I ask, the disbelief clawing up my throat now. "Do you even hear yourself?"

"I'm trying," he snaps. "You think I don't see what's happening? You're different. Ever since that mark appeared. Ever since *he* showed up."

My pulse jumps.

"You think I didn't notice the way you looked at him after you were marked? When *he* brought you home?" Rhys sneers, stepping forward. "You don't say anything, but I'm not stupid. I see it. You don't look at me like that. I don't think you ever have."

"Don't," I say, voice hardening.

"I was your husband first," he says, a bitter edge cutting through. "You were mine before all this fate-marked bullshit twisted everything."

"You never acted like I was yours," I say, and the words hang in the air like a slap.

He stares at me. For the first time in forever, he doesn't have a reply.

"I don't know what I ever meant to you, Rhys," I continue, quieter now. "But this—this isn't love. This is ownership. And I'm not for sale."

Della steps into the room like she owns the air—at this point, I wouldn't be surprised if she does. A swirl of cinnamon and storm follows her, and somehow, her boots don't make a sound on the floor.

"I brought you tea," she says, walking straight past Rhys as though he's not even there to hand me the mug. "You're vibrating."

Rhys scowls. "Hi to you too, Della."

"Yeah, I don't like conversing with the enemy," she responds.

"Seriously?" His eyes widen. "You've known me for five minutes."

"And in that five minutes, I watched you try to manipulate the woman you claim to love into selling the only thing that's actually hers." She folds her arms, cocking her head. "So, yeah. That earned you a category."

He lets out a short laugh. "Unbelievable. You don't know what we've been through."

"I don't have to," Della says, unbothered. "I know what I walked into. I know a power play when I hear one. And I know you're terrified of losing control now that she's starting to think for herself."

"Bella," Rhys says. "You're really going to let her turn you against me?"

I open my mouth, but Della beats me to it. "She didn't need my help, sweetheart," she says with a grin. "You did that all on your own."

Rhys lunges.

His hand wraps around her arm before I can move, his face twisted in something that's not heartbreak—it's humiliation.

"What the hell do you think you know?" he growls. "I don't know who you think you are, but you're not part of this. This is between Bella and I."

Della tilts her head, eyes narrowing.

"Bad move," she mutters. In one clean motion, she grabs his wrist, twists hard, and drives her knee up—straight into his gut.

Rhys wheezes and doubles over.

She moves. Boots silent on tile. An elbow to his ribs followed by an open-palm strike to the shoulder, and he goes sprawling into the bookshelf.

Rhys tries to rise. But Della kicks his leg out and stares at his form on the floor.

"I know what you did," she snarls, looming over him now. "The deal. The lies. The gaslighting. I know *everything*."

He spits blood onto the floor. "You think you're better than me?"

"No," she says, crouching low, eyes burning copper. "I *am* better than you. And she deserves someone who won't turn her love into a fucking chokehold."

She straightens, slowly, breathing hard—but still poised. "You're lucky she's here," she says, glaring down at him. "Because I was two seconds away from cracking your jaw."

Rhys glares up at her, breathing shallow, humiliated.

"You touch her again," Della adds, voice low and final, "and I won't stop next time."

She turns to me, eyes softening. "You okay?"

I nod, stunned. Shaking. "Yeah. I am now."

Rhys pulls himself up, groaning, clutching his side. His eyes flick to me—something desperate, wounded. But I don't move.

"You should go," I say, voice flat.

"This isn't over, Bella. I love you and I'm not giving up. Not on us. Not ever." He walks out before another word can be said, slamming the door so hard the painting my sister gave me rattles against the wall.

"Well that was fun. Ready to file for divorce? Maybe you can still get an annulment!" Della exclaims in a frighteningly happy way.

"Okay Della... I think that's enough caffeine for you today," I chuckle.

"Hey," she says, softening her voice in an irritating way. "What's that face?"

I shake my head, sitting on my desk chair. Crossing my legs, I throw my head back and sigh. "I just... I don't know. I feel like a failure," I murmur. "I married him. I said yes. I stood there and promised forever. And now, what—months later, I'm walking away? Just like that?"

"You chose safety," Della says gently. "You chose what looked like perfection. That's not weakness, Bella."

I shake my head. "But I knew. Somewhere deep down—I knew he wasn't it."

"And you stayed anyway," she says. "Because you thought love was earned. That if you gave enough, it would eventually be returned."

My chest aches.

"You don't earn real love," Della goes on. "It meets you where you are."

I look away. "And Owen?"

"Owen isn't wild or reckless." Della's eyes flicker. "He's the gravity that holds everything together when it should fall apart. He's endured things that would hollow most men."

She leans in.

"You were made for each other in a way that has nothing to do with destiny," Della continues.

I shift uncomfortably, staring down at my hands. "I don't even know him," I admit. "Not really. Just that night. A few minutes the morning after. I haven't spoken to him since."

Della lifts an eyebrow. "So speak to him."

I glance up, confused. "You mean—?"

"Use the bond," she says simply. "That mark burning across your skin? It's not just decoration. It's a door. Try knocking."

I shake my head. "What would I even say?"

"Hi," she says dryly. "That's usually a start."

A tiny laugh escapes me before I can stop it.

Della leans closer. "You don't have to know how it ends, Bella. You just have to choose to begin."

I sigh and breathe out. *Here goes nothing.*

Arabella: *Owen? Can you hear me?*

Owen: *Arabella? Are you okay?*

His voice slides through my mind like fine wine—rich, smooth, and impossibly grounding.

"He answered me," I say, looking suddenly at Della.

"Okay. I think it's time I leave. Bye. Let me know how it goes!" She sing-songs as she walks out.

"Wait! But–" I'm cut off by the slamming of the door.

Owen: *Are you still there?*

Arabella: *Yeah. Sorry. Della was leaving.*

I can hear his chuckle through the link.

Owen: *She is an interesting human to say the least.*

Arabella: *She is.*

Owen: *What did you want to talk about, Sweetheart?*

I like that. The way he says Sweetheart. Rhys never said those names. He never made me feel this way the few times he did.

Arabella: *I want to get to know you.*

Owen: *Okay. When?*

"Hey, Bella," a voice calls, bright and familiar.

Josie Brighton leans through the doorway, her blonde curls are barely contained in a lopsided bun. She's wearing a red crochet sweater with pink butterflies stitched across the shoulders, paired with worn jeans and purple Converse covered in glitter. Classic Josie: chaotic, kind, and somehow always put together in the exact way kids adore.

She holds up a hot pink folder. "Lesson plans. Also, I added an edible playdough recipe. Don't ask why. Just... trust me."

I smile despite the weight in my chest. "I always do."

Josie walks in fully and collapses into the chair across from my desk with a dramatic sigh. "These children are tiny agents of chaos, and I love them, but one more glue stick incident and I will walk straight into the ocean."

"You say that every week," I reply.

"And I mean it every week," she says, grinning. Then her eyes sharpen a bit. "Now, tell me why you look like you haven't slept since last Thursday."

"I've been busy," I say, sighing and deflating just enough for her to notice.

"You've been disappearing," she corrects. "And your busy face is dangerously close to your emotional crisis face."

I give a tired laugh. "It's complicated."

Josie softens. "I'm your friend first, coworker second, nosy preschool fairy godmother third. You can tell me if the world's falling apart, you know?"

"It's Rhys..." I start.

"Enough said," she groans.

Josie has never liked Rhys. Like me, she sees my vision here. She's here for it. She also hates that Rhys is trying to take that away.

Owen: *I can feel you're busy.*

Shit. I completely forgot about Owen. He didn't sound mad at least.

Arabella: *Yeah. I'm working. Rain check?*

Owen: *You know how to reach me. Go save the world, sweetheart.*

He understands. No questions asked or anger.

"We have a situation," Colene, our front desk Social Worker, says.

Her clipboard is clutched tight to her chest, her expression carved in urgency.

Josie and I both straighten immediately.

"Single mother, two kids," Colene says quickly. "Referral from CPS just came in. Domestic violence case. They need emergency placement tonight."

Josie is already standing. "Ages?"

"I don't know for sure, but I think maybe three or four, then possibly one, but possibly younger. Two boys," Colene answers.

"I've got the playroom prepped. I'll take them," Josie says without hesitation, already heading for the door.

"Thank you," I call after her.

Colene turns to me. "Mom's shaken but holding it together. She's in the lobby. Housing's prepping Apartment 3B for a midnight placement, but we'll need to fast-track the paperwork. Are you good to take point?"

"I've got her," I say, grabbing the folder from my desk and slinging my sweater over my arm. "Let's do it."

The mother's standing just inside the doorway of the lobby, stiff with exhaustion, arms curled protectively around a toddler who's half-asleep against her chest. The older little boy clings to her hand with both of his. He doesn't cry. Just watches everything, like he's memorizing the exits.

Her coat is zipped halfway, a fruit pouch tucked awkwardly in the pocket. One of her shoes is untied. Her hair's been pulled into a quick knot, the kind you make when you're running out the door and it keeps getting in the way.

The woman looks to be in her early twenties. Her eyes flick to me warily before scanning the rest of the room behind me, like she's scanning for a trap.

Behind her, the caseworker gives me a quick nod. Her name tag reads A. Mendez, and her eyes are kind but tired. She's seen too many stories that look like this one.

I take a step forward and say softly, "You're safe now. Let's get you settled."

"Can I take them?" Josie asks, stepping up behind us.

"I... I don't know," she quivers. I can see she's shaking and gripping her toddler tighter.

"I promise they will be safe with Josie. She is our teacher and there is a fully equipped playroom. We don't want them to hear this." I wait for her to make a decision. She looks like she's never been afforded that opportunity before.

"Okay, but not for long," she says, giving Josie a stern look.

She looks her oldest in the eye, brushing his curls back. "Mama just has to talk to the nice lady for a little bit, okay? You're going to stay with Miss Josie, and she's going to play with you and your brother. I'll be right back. Promise."

She presses a kiss to his temple and next to the baby's forehead. "Be brave for me. Just for a little while."

They go off to Josie's domain holding her hand and chattering, leaving us alone.

"How about we head to my office?" I hold out my arm to lead the way.

She hesitates for a second and I immediately know what she's thinking. She doesn't want to leave her kids to strangers.

"My office is just next to the playroom. There is a window where you'll still be able to see the kids through it."

She nods and follows without a word, her shoulders are hunched like she's trying to make herself smaller. No matter how many times I see women doing the exact same thing, it always breaks my heart.

I tried to make my office a safe haven. Something soft around the edges, especially when the rest of their world feels hard. A worn velvet loveseat sits in the corner with a knit throw blanket draped over it, instead of a stiff metal chair. Calming sage and lavender incense burn low in the ceramic holder by the window. I keep the lights dim on purpose—too many overhead fluorescents feel like an interrogation.

She sits like she's not sure she's allowed to.

"Would you feel comfortable telling us what happened?" I ask, keeping my voice as comforting as possible. "Whatever you're ready to share."

"My name's Tiana Holloway. I'm twenty-three. My boys are Malakai and Ezra. Kai's three. Ezra just turned one."

She doesn't look at either of us when she says it—just stares at her hands.

"I met Shawn when I was seventeen. He was older. Said I was mature for my age. That I needed someone to take care of me. That I was special." Tiana scoffs under her breath, but there's no humor in it.

"He was sweet at first. That kind of sweet that makes you second guess every red flag. But that didn't last long and it turned fast. He became the most possessive person you'd ever meet. He didn't want me talking to anyone. Said my mom was toxic, my friends were jealous, my coworkers were flirting."

Her fingers twitch in her lap.

"By the time I realized what it was, I was already pregnant with Kai. And that's when he really changed. Started throwing things. Spitting in my food. Calling me names I wouldn't repeat in front of my kids. He'd take my keys so I couldn't leave. Smash my phone. Once, he took Ezra's formula and dumped it down the sink, just to make a point."

I feel my hands clench in my lap.

"He'd tell Kai to shut up when he cried. Push him out of the way if he was standing too close. I started sleeping with my kids in my arms just so I'd know they were still breathing in the morning."

Tiana finally looks up with tears in her eyes. "I never thought I'd be the girl who stays. But when you've got no money, no contact with your family, and two babies... staying feels a lot safer than facing life on the streets."

She glances at Mendez, who gives her the smallest nod of encouragement.

"I tried to leave once before. Packed a bag and hid it in the closet. He found it. Beat me so bad I couldn't stand for two days. Told me if I ever ran again, he'd take the boys and I'd never see them."

Her next words come out brittle.

"I believed him."

She starts choking and I immediately grab her some water from the fridge next to my desk.

"Three nights ago, he got drunk. Started screaming because dinner was cold. I told him I didn't care. That he didn't scare me anymore." She shakes her head. "I shouldn't have said it. But I did."

She pulls up her sleeve slightly—just enough to show bruises along her arm.

"Kai jumped in front of me. Said 'don't hurt my mommy.' He's three. And he was trying to protect me."

She wipes at her eyes roughly.

"I waited until he passed out. Grabbed the diaper bag, both boys, and ran. Mendez picked us up from the gas station."

I finally speak. "You did the right thing."

"I don't know what happens next," Tiana says. "But I can't go back. I don't care what he says. I'll die before I let him get near my sons again."

"You don't have to go back," I say gently. "You're safe now. Both of them are too."

By the time the last intake form is signed and the apartment's stocked with blankets, snacks, and toothpaste, it's past 1AM. The center is empty now. Well except for the night staff.

Tiana's settled. The kids are asleep. And for the first time all day, I let myself relax.

My bones ache. My eyes swell. My soul feels like it's been wrung out and left to dry on a wire.

The last thing I should do is reach out to him.

But I do.

Arabella: *Owen? I have some time now. Open to that rain check?*

No reply.

I sigh, leaning back and closing my eyes.

When I open them again, he's here. Standing in my office. No knock or warning. Just Owen in black slacks and sin, his smile is pure male pride.

"You don't have to ask twice," he says, voice rough like gravel soaked in whiskey. "You think about me and I'll be here."

Chapter Four
Owen

I heard her call and before I knew it, I was standing in her office. Feeling giddy. *Really? Giddy?*

"You don't have to ask twice," I say. I can hear how gravely my voice sounds. "You think about me and I'll be here."

"Well, I'm glad you came. Today has been a day." She smiles, but there's something behind her eyes betraying her tone.

"Do tell. What happened today?" I ask. I'm genuinely curious.

That startles me a bit. I've never asked anyone how their day was or even cared for that matter.

"New intake. We're lucky we had an apartment available. She is running from her abusive life at home. Wanting a new start," she sighs.

"See but that's not really what's bothering you. That's your job. One that you've done every day for years. Why was this one so bad?"

"Ah you caught that huh. Maybe I understand the running away she's trying to do. I feel the same way. Actually about Rhys in a way. That when I married him, I was running away or something. Weird I know, but true," she says honestly.

"Weird?" I echo. "No. It's honest."

She looks at me like she wasn't expecting that—like people usually let her shrug this kind of thing off. I'm taking every clue that she'll give me, I want to take every bad moment, every worry, every stress from her that I can. I want to give her comfort, love, peace, anything that she could ever possibly want.

"Come on," she says after a moment. "Let's go to my place. I need to get off my feet, and you," her lips twitch slightly, "look like you're itching to ask more questions."

"I might be," I admit, falling into step behind her.

Going back to her place takes me back to that night. When I brought her home.

"Sorry it's a mess," she says, brushing hair off her forehead.

"Don't apologize," I say. "It's good."

She hands me a glass of wine and sinks onto the couch like she's been holding up the sky.

"Tell me what you're really thinking," I say, sitting beside her.

She hesitates. Just for a second.

"I'm thinking about life. That I'm lucky to even have one. The women I help. The kids. They aren't as lucky as me. But for some reason, I'm drawn to it. And sometimes I feel like that makes me uncomfortable. Am I doing this for me... or for them?"

I lean forward, glass untouched. "Maybe it's both. Maybe the thing that makes you powerful isn't that you give until it hurts. Maybe it's that you keep showing up. Even when no one else does. Even when it breaks you open."

I turn to look at her. Directly into her eyes. I want to make sure that she hears me. Every word. "That doesn't make you selfish—it makes you necessary."

She swallows hard. I can see it in her eyes—how long she's carried that question, unsure who she'd be without it.

"You don't owe anyone anything. You are trying to carry everyone else's feelings. Just think about your own."

"Enough about me. Let's talk about you," she says, sighing.

Now I don't know what to say. She has this way of catching me off guard. I never talk about me, but who better to start with than my soulmate.

"That's a dangerous thing to talk about with a man like me," I chuckle.

"I like living on the edge," she says. "Tell me about the deals. What's it like?"

I raise a brow. "What, you want the sales pitch?"

She shrugs, curling her legs beneath her on the couch, facing me fully, her emerald eyes shine with curiosity. "Maybe. Or the fine print. Do demons offer warranties?"

A laugh slips out of me. "No, no. I don't do takebacks. One-time offer." I lean back, studying her. "People make deals for all kinds of reasons—desperation, grief, ego, love. Sometimes just to feel something."

Her brows lift slightly, but she doesn't interrupt.

"Thing is," I continue, "I never lie. I don't twist arms. I just hold up the mirror. They look, and they decide what they're willing to give."

She tilts her head, voice soft but pointed. "And you take it?"

"I used to," I admit, the words coming slower now. "Took everything they offered. Greedy, right?" I wiggle my brows at her with a mischievous grin.

There's the flicker of a smile. on her stunning face, but it fades when I add, "But lately... I don't know. I think I've had enough of carrying other people's wreckage."

"So if you're not taking deals anymore..." she asks, quiet but curious, "where does that leave you? In the future, I mean?"

The future's always been a revolving door of bargains and signatures. People desperate for miracles. People willing to trade away the pieces they should've held onto. And me, always there with the pen.

"I don't know," I admit. "I was born for this. Raised in it. You know Julian stepped back from it. Doesn't make deals anymore."

She tilts her head, listening, her arms curled around her knees.

"He handles collection now," I say. "When a contract ends, he finds the soul and delivers it to our mother. Sometimes Aunt Selene helps. It's less frequent. More structured. He's still in the game—but on his terms."

I glance over at her. "Means he can be with Ophelia more. They travel. They're building things together."

And I envy him for it.

Not the power. Not the prestige.

The choice. The life.

"I've never let myself imagine stepping away," I murmur. "But now... I'm starting to think maybe I don't want to be the one people fear anymore. Maybe I want to be the reason someone smiles."

Her eyes soften and her fingers twitch like she might reach for me, but she doesn't. Not yet.

And still, I find myself talking.

"You know, I used to think love was a weakness. That it clouded judgment, dulled the edges. But Julian—he's still him. Just grounded in some way. Like she gave him a center of gravity." I look back at her. "And maybe that's what I want too. Not to change who I am. But to have something, someone, that keeps me grounded enough to choose who I want to be."

We keep talking—about nothing and everything. Her favorite childhood book. The first time I realized I could manipulate time in a deal. How she can't cook unless there's a playlist on, preferably soul music or moody indie. I tell her how I once collected a soul from a cursed vineyard in the south of France, and she tells me how

Hearthlight used to be an old convent turned shelter. The words are easy, and so are the moments where we don't talk between them.

But somewhere around 3AM, her posture shifts. Her voice slows. She finishes her third glass of wine and sets it down carefully.

I read the signs.

"I think it's time I head out," I say gently. "You need sleep."

She nods, but doesn't move. "Probably for the best," she murmurs. "But I don't want this to be over."

"Over?" I echo, confused.

Her tired eyes meet mine. "Our time together. I like this. I like you. It feels right."

Something tightens in my chest.

"I think I'm going to get a divorce, Owen," she adds, voice shaking slightly.

She lets out a breath, and something in her shoulders eases. "I'll walk you out," she says.

But she doesn't, one second she's watching me and the next, her lips are on mine. The most intense and incredible feeling rushes through my body. The best I've felt in a long time.

Her breath stumbles. Her hand flies to her mouth. "Shit. I—Owen, I didn't mean to—I mean, I did, but..."

"You don't have to explain," I say quietly. She is quickly becoming my everything. She also would never hurt anyone. Not intentionally anyway.

Her eyes brim with guilt. "I'm still married. That was—"

"Real," I finish for her. "But if you need space, I'll give it."

She closes her eyes like the room is spinning. "I'm sorry."

"Don't be," I say, pulling my brows together. "You're allowed to want more."

I turn to leave and she doesn't stop me.

I don't wait another second. I go straight to Hell. Not home, but to my parent's house. I need to investigate Rhys. Do what Della recommended. It's time to finish this once and for all.

"Mom! Are you home?" I shout, slamming the door behind me.

The wards shiver in response, but it's not mom who answers first.

"Yelling won't make her move faster," Selene drawls from the sunken couch, legs curled beneath her like a cat with claws.

I spot her swirling something dark in a chalice that looks older than most empires.

"She home or not?" I ask, already pacing.

"She's coming," Theron calls from the hallway, his voice like gravel and dusk. "Try not to shatter anything while we wait."

My mom appears then, barefoot and calm, a long robe cinched at the waist, moonlight practically stitched into the fabric. Her eyes flick to me. "You only scream like that when something's broken. Or when you've done the breaking."

"It's not me," I say, voice tight. "It's Bella. It's Rhys. I need help."

That earns their attention.

Selene sits up straighter. "Finally," she says. "A problem I can sink my teeth into."

Liora folds her arms. "Speak."

"There's something about him. I know he's working with the Creeds, but there's more to it." I pace around the room needing to do *something*.

Footsteps echoed behind me.

My father, Evander's, voice grunts. "We dig deeper. We don't let this fester."

Owen: *Julian... I need you and Ophelia.*

I send the thought with precision. Or I think I do.

Minutes later, Julian steps into the room, Ophelia trailing close behind. She says nothing, eyes scanning the space like she's waiting for it to turn on her. Smart.

Julian arches a brow. "Didn't expect the summons."

"I didn't summon," I correct. "I requested." A grin creeps its way onto my face.

"Right." He glances around and rolls his eyes. "You always request with that tone."

Lucas is the next to walk in, smirking like he's already read the punchline.

"I knew you loved us," he says, voice dry. "Didn't expect you to admit it in broadcast."

I freeze. Check the link I cast. Dammit.

Seth saunters in, all teeth and mischief. "Owen, babe, if you wanted the whole family to drop everything, you could've just said so. Group chat would've sufficed."

Caleb strolls in behind him with a drink. "Is this an emergency? Or just emotionally repressed bonding? Either way, I'm in."

Damian appears without a word, scanning the room like he's expecting an enemy.

Adrian follows, expression unreadable. "You called all of us," he says, tone flat. "That's not like you."

"I didn't mean to," I mutter.

"You tried to be subtle," Julian says. "Didn't work."

I pinch the bridge of my nose. "I was aiming for precision. Apparently, I hit everyone."

Theron slides into the conversation with a wide grin. "Classic slip. Happens to the best of us. Usually after a bottle of something strong."

Selene appears with her ever-calm voice. "Sometimes the universe delivers who you need, not who you intended."

"You're going to look into Rhys, aren't you?" Ophelia glances at me. Straight to the point.

"Yeah. Something needs to be done about him," I concede.

"Right. What do you have so far?" Julian asks.

"Only what Della told me. That he is working with the Creeds," I say.

Lucas cracks his neck. "I'll sniff out where he's been. If he's made moves in our circles, someone will remember. Even if they'd rather not."

"I'll check the damage," Seth says, with a little bit too much enthusiasm if I'm being honest. "Power like that leaves bruises on places. People. I'll see who's limping."

Caleb nods once and rubs his hands together. "I'll tap into the favors he's called in. Who's covering for him. Who's suddenly rich or scared."

Adrian leans forward, voice cool. "I'll go quiet. See who starts talking when they think no one's listening."

"I'll follow his rhythm," Damian adds. "Everyone has one. I'll find where his broke."

Julian looks at me. "You?"

"I'll stay. Della's coming to us."

Ophelia lifts a brow. "She trusts you."

"She doesn't have a choice," I say.

No one needs to say more.

They vanish one by one. Gone like knives into dark water.

"How do you think I call Della?" I ask Ophelia. Her and Julian were the only two that stayed behind.

"I know you said that she needs to come to us, but what if you went to Hex & Brews? Talk to her there," she responds.

"Sounds good to me," I say, getting up and heading for the door.

Hex & Brews doesn't advertise itself. It doesn't need to. Set into a quiet corner of the city with ivy climbing the brick, the black door gleams like it's been freshly polished, and the brass plaque reads HEX & BREWS. NO LIES. NO FANGS. NO TAB.

I open the door, step inside and instantly feel it.

The air smells like fresh brewed tea, cardamom, old magic, and something uniquely hers—like clove and citrus. Floating lights drift overhead like lazy fireflies. The walls are lined with stacked books, dried herbs, and curated chaos. The kind that only works because someone powerful willed it to. This isn't just a café. It's a sanctuary. Every inch of it humming with intentional magic.

The menu above the copper bar shifts between hand-scripted blends. Spelled Chai. Truth Serum Tonic. Heartbreak Hibiscus. Blood Orange Black. There's something called Memory Fog Oolong, and another just labeled Don't Ask, Just Sip. Wards pulse faintly under every table. The vines curling along the ceiling feel alive, but at ease.

And somehow... so am I.

I breathe in. For the first time all day, the tension in my shoulders loosens.

I love it here. Not that I say it out loud.

I feel them before I hear them. The parade of my family telling me what they found out about Rhys.

Lucas: *He's been laundering money for them—Creed-backed shell groups disguised as nonprofits. Community investment, education grants, redevelopment. All fake. All channels to bleed power without getting noticed.*

Seth: *He's been silencing small voices. Not violently—strategically. Investigative "oversight," delays in publishing, quiet discrediting campaigns. He controls the story before it ever breaks.*

Caleb: *He's not a new recruit. He's been working with the Creeds since the Cassius Arden expose. Back when they needed a new face—clean, moral, relentless. Rhys was their answer. And their asset.*

Adrian: *He used his reporting to bury competitors. Dismantle resistance. Anyone who got close to Creed deals? Their names got smeared in op-eds. In "anonymous sources." In features that sounded like truth.*

Damian: *He's twisted public perception around Bella for months. Soft narratives. Quiet concern. Headlines that frame her as overwhelmed, underqualified. So when she sells, it'll look like grace. Not betrayal.*

Owen: *He was sent to win her.*

Julian: *It was strategic. Seduce her. Marry her. Earn her trust, then hand Hearthlight to the Creeds on a silver fucking platter. They wanted the land, the energy, the influence. Bella was just the gateway.*

Owen: *Only problem? He actually fell for her. Somewhere in the middle of the lies, he caught real feelings. Now he's stuck. Still reporting. Still feeding them. But tangled up in guilt and love like that's going to fix it.*

I sit perfectly still at the bar, letting each thread settle.

Della steps into view from the back, eyes on me.

"Bad news?" she asks.

"Worse."

"I'm assuming you know everything now," she says, it's not a question.

"I do." My jaw is set as I nod.

She leans on the bar. "He's not going away."

"No." I shake my head. "He thinks he's in love."

"That's the dangerous part." Her tone is clipped, dry. "He doesn't see betrayal. Just sacrifice. Romance. Like he's the tragic one."

"He believes if he explains it right, she'll agree with him and forgive him. Everything will go back to normal."

She pours tea with slow precision, then slides the cup toward me without meeting my eyes. "He still wants her. Still thinks he deserves her."

"If she believes him..." I let the words die.

"She won't," Della says, completely convinced. "Not after what she sees."

"She trusted him," I murmur.

Her gaze cuts to mine. "She will trust you too. I'll be there, Julian and Ophelia too. She'll believe all of us."

I nod once. The tension in my chest doesn't ease. "It has to come from all of us."

"Agreed." Her fingers drum lightly on the counter. "No confusion. No space for him to twist it."

"He's going to fight for her."

Della's mouth curves, but there's no humor in it. "We won't let him win."

Chapter Five
Arabella

My phone rings for what feels like the thousandth time. *Seriously, Rhys?*

Owen left around 3AM last night and it's almost noon now. I don't want to talk to Rhys. Not after what he did to Della, but I know I have to.

I can't stop thinking about the kiss with Owen. I didn't mean to do it. I just did it. On instinct. It was a pull that I haven't felt in a very long time. Truthfully, I don't know if I ever really felt that with Rhys.

My phone buzzes. I open the message without thinking, then immediately curse myself in my head.

Rhys

Can we talk? Please.

I stare at the screen, thumb hesitating.

I'm not ready.

His response is instant.

Rhys

Just five minutes. In person. That's all I'm asking.

I close my eyes and exhale slowly.

Fine. But I'm at work.

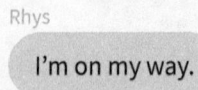

Rhys

I'm on my way.

I sit with the ache in my chest and the memory of Owen's mouth still lingering on mine.

I know I can call Ophelia—if I need her, she'll be here in a blink of an eye, without another thought.

It's just that I want to figure this out by myself this time, not because I don't need her, but because I don't want to completely rely on her. She took care of me most of our lives, but now... she has one of her own. I want her to have that. Not having to carry mine too.

I don't have time to even breathe before a portal opens up and in walks the last people I thought I would see today.

Owen, Julian, and Della, but Ophelia is the one that I'm the most excited to see.

I wrap my arms around her like I've been holding it together just long enough to fall apart here. We're still close, even though she lives the majority of the time in Hell.

"What are you guys doing here?" I ask, grinning like a fool.

"For you. After everything that has happened in our lives, we're always here for each other," Ophelia starts. "How is everything between you and Rhys? Especially now that you're mated."

"I got it handled, Lia." I cross my arms, blurting that out too fast. I don't want her to know about everything. Part of me is embarrassed about that.

"Did you ever tell Rosalind that you're married?"

My mom. She's in the Maldives right now. The last I heard, anyway.

Ever since everything happened with our father, she's been floating—jet-setting from country to country like if she moves fast enough, the past won't stick.

She's wonderful. Free-spirited. Fierce. But she's not the one I go to when my life falls apart.

Not like Ophelia.

"No," I admit. "I think part of me is questioning every decision I made. Like... how did I let it get this far?"

Ophelia squeezes my hand. "You were trying to believe in something good. That doesn't make you weak."

Before I can answer, Della's voice cuts clean through the moment. "We've got more pressing matters," she says from across the room. "And not enough time."

I glance at her. Her gaze is fixed on the door. Jaw tight. Fingers twitching like she's already prepping a spell.

"He's coming," she adds.

Everything inside me goes still. "Who's coming?" I ask.

"Rhys," Della responds.

"Oh, yeah." I blow out a breath, I almost forgot that he was coming in. "We're going to talk."

"Then we're here at the perfect time. Because we need to talk to you first," Della says. "Ophelia? Do you want to say it?"

"No," she says. "I think Owen needs to be the one to tell her."

"Tell me what?" I shoot them all a look.

"They brought Rhys in to take down Cassius Arden," Owen says. "The Creeds wanted him out of the way so Ellison could move in on the mayoral bid. Rhys was their secret weapon. A journalist with a conscience. Or so it looked."

My chest tightens.

"He tried to come at it sideways—approached Ophelia first. Tried to get her to hand over dirt for an exposé. When she didn't give him anything..." Owen's eyes lock on mine. He doesn't blink. "They sent him after you."

My mouth goes dry.

"They wanted Hearthlight," he says, voice low. "For money."

I blink. "Money?"

"The developers have been circling for years," I say. "But I thought it was background noise—distraction while we protected the land."

Owen shakes his head. "This wasn't about rezoning—it was a full acquisition plan. Hidden shell companies. Private offers. Suppression contracts buried in modernization language. Rhys would get his cut, of course."

I can't breathe.

"He was supposed to make you fall for him," Owen continues. "Marry you. Earn your trust. Then guide you to sell."

A cold, sick anvil drops into my stomach.

"He's been sleeping with his coworker," Owen adds, the look on his face says he knows the hurt I'm feeling right now. "For most of your marriage. Only ended recently. And not because of guilt...because she pulled back when the Creeds started pressuring him harder."

"How?" I whisper.

"By writing an exposé on Talia and Stellan Rothwell. Twisted their story. Sold it to people who wanted them ruined. All for a quick buy-in. One more favor. One more paycheck. He says he fell in love with you. That it's real."

I want to laugh. Scream. Fold in half. "Was it?" I ask.

Owen's gaze doesn't soften. "It was transactional," he says. "All of it."

I try to process this. Owen didn't sugarcoat anything. Not that I wanted him to. But damn. This is... a lot.

"Okay, well that makes my final decision to divorce him that much easier," I say.

I'm not someone who second-guesses. I hate the back and forth of it. Always have.

But Rhys? He made me do that constantly. For over a year, I've been spinning in circles, questioning my instincts, biting back things I knew were right. He made doubt feel like loyalty.

No more.

My office door flies open and in storms Rhys. "I tried to stop at Hex & Brews so Della could make your special, but she wasn't there—" He freezes when he sees them.

"What the fuck are you doing here?" His voice rises as he stalks toward Owen.

"Stop!" I shout, stepping between them. "They were just informing me about your indiscretions."

Rhys freezes. His eyes dart back to me. "What are you talking about?"

I fold my arms. "Don't play dumb."

"I'm not—" He takes a half step closer, hands raised like he's calming a child. "Bella, I don't even know what they told you, but whatever it is—"

"They told me everything," I say. "The Creeds. Hearthlight. The affair. Talia and Stellan. You've been working this long before I ever knew you."

"No, wait—that's not—this is all twisted." He gestures wildly toward Owen. "They're spinning it. You know how they are."

"Oh, so now you're the victim?" I snap. "Is that the play?"

"I never wanted it to be like this," he says, voice dropping. "I didn't mean for it to go so far. I fell for you, Bella. I swear I did."

"But you still only care about yourself," I respond.

Rhys flinches. "No. You don't get it. I was trying to protect you."

I stare at him. "From what? The truth?"

"From losing everything," he says, voice rising again. "You don't know how the Creeds work. They don't make deals, they make threats. I thought if I could get close—if I could keep things calm—they'd back off. I was trying to protect Hearthlight."

"You married me to protect *your position*."

He steps closer, hands out. "I stayed because I love you."

"Yet you cheated on me," I choke out, the words burning as they leave my throat.

"That is not true," Rhys says, too fast.

"You're seriously going to stand there and deny it?" I ask, incredulous.

His jaw tightens. "You have no proof. You're just listening to suspicion," he growls, trying to get back some semblance of control.

"I have proof," Della says, stepping forward, her tone icy.

She hands me a slim file, and when I open it, my breath catches. Photos of Rhys and a woman. Close. Intimate. Kissing in some, meeting in hidden corners in others.

I hold one up.

"I think I have my proof now," I say with a humorless laugh.

Rhys lunges forward and rips them out of my hands. "Where did you get these?"

"Where you left your integrity." She walks up to Rhys, getting right in his face.

I step beside Della, not raising my voice. "I want a divorce."

Rhys freezes, his mouth parting like I've just knocked the breath from his lungs. "You don't mean that," he says, voice cracking at the edges.

"I've never meant anything more." The words taste bitter in my mouth.

He just stares at me, eyes wide like he still can't believe I'd say it. Like I'm the one who broke something.

I almost laugh.

Because I gave him everything—my trust, my loyalty, the kind of love you choose to fight for. He chipped away at it piece by piece, all while smiling like nothing was wrong.

My hands curl at my sides. I won't cry. Not in front of him. It aches in a way that feels like something inside me is folding in on itself.

"The thing that hurts," I say solemnly, "is that I meant it. Every part of it. Even when you didn't."

He opens his mouth again, but I don't want to hear it. I know the tears will come—later, when I'm alone and no one's watching. But not now. Now, I'm going to walk away with what I have left, with my chin held high.

"Just leave," I whisper.

"This isn't over," he spits before storming out of the room like he was the one wronged.

"Always needs the last word," Della scoffs.

I turn to look at my family—the people who stood by me, protected me, loved me, even when I lost my way.

"I don't have the words to thank you," I say softly.

"You don't need words," Ophelia says, stepping forward. "We're your family. That's the whole point."

"Besides," Della adds with a faint smirk, "you'd do the same for us. With more dramatics, probably."

I huff a laugh, but it catches when Owen steps behind me and wraps his arms around my waist, pulling me gently against him.

"Hate to break this up, but maybe we can talk about next steps," Julian finally speaks up.

"Divorce," I finish the blanks that no one wants to say. "Anyone know an attorney?"

"We might," Julian says. "What about Raymond Ellery?"

"Ellery?" Owen asks. "Does he even do divorces?"

"Doesn't hurt to ask," Julian shrugs.

Flopping down on the couch in my apartment, I send a text to Josie, letting her know that I had to go home and I just need some time. She's amazing and I know she'll keep everything afloat, but right now, I can't afford anyone to be walking in on us... summoning a demon.

Once we're all in the living room, I close and lock my front door.

"Okay," I start. "What's his number? Can we call him?"

"Already did," Julian states, completely deadpan. "He'll be here in a minute."

A ripple begins to float through the air as a man, Raymond Ellery, steps through a portal that appeared in the middle of my apartment.

He brushes a speck off of the lapel on his light grey suit as if this was just another Tuesday morning and not the end of my marriage.

"Someone mentioned a divorce," he says in a cool tone. "Thought it would be best to bring reinforcements."

He glances behind him as a woman steps through next. Her dark brown hair is smoothly pulled back and her hazel eyes are slightly eerie.

"Julia Carver," Raymond says, stepping aside. "Senior partner at my firm. She's human—which makes her uniquely qualified to handle certain... mortal complexities."

"Let's get started, shall we?" She asks, gesturing to the couch.

I sit with Owen on one side and Ophelia on the other.

"I'd love to stay, but I really have to get back to work," Della says. "I love you, Bella. I'll talk to you later."

She disappears as quickly as she comes. Leaving Julian, Ophelia, Owen, and I. Which is weird if you think about it. So I just won't.

I watch as Julia sits across from me, pulling a leather notepad out of her bag and taking out her pen. Jeez, she's intense.

"Let's start with the basics. Timeline. Date of marriage. Anything he pressured you into signing?" She asks, all business.

I rattle off everything that she asks, barely paying attention.

Raymond glances at Julia. "Coercion and conflict of interest are on the table. We could push for an annulment, but the affair gives us solid footing for dissolution with asset protections."

"No," I cut in. My voice is shriller than I expected, making me jump in the process. "Divorce. I want it done. I don't need to erase what happened. I just want to end it. But I don't want him to have any room to rewrite the story. I absolutely do not want him to have Hearthlight."

Julia nods, sharply. "Our next move is to file for immediate legal separation. If needed, we can get you temporary protection orders. We'll also need a statement detailing any manipulation or pressure to sell Hearthlight."

"We can use that?" I ask.

"He married you under false pretenses," Julia says, lifting a brow. "That's leverage."

"We will destroy him so he doesn't have a leg to stand on. You will walk away and be able to spend time with your soulmate," Raymond smirks.

"How did you know?" I ask, chuckling.

Raymond tugs his collar aside, revealing a mark of his own on his chest.

"Well that explains... everything," I say, smiling.

He has a soulmate too. He understands.

"Okay. Paperwork's done." Julia stands while brushing imaginary wrinkles off of her slacks. "I will get this filed first thing in the morning."

She and Raymond portal out as soon as they shake our hands. Here's to hoping this all goes without a hitch and I never have to see Rhys again, but that's too easy for my life.

"That's our cue," Julian says with a crooked smile.

"We're just a thought way if you need us," Ophelia adds, her eyes lingering on mine with the older sister wisdom that I know all too well. She's making sure that I'm going to be okay.

They leave and it's just Owen and I. He doesn't speak at first. Just sighs and pulls me deeper into his embrace.

In his arms, everything stops spinning. My heart stops bracing for the next blow. For the first time in forever... I feel safe.

Chapter Six
Owen

A date, We're going on a date. It feels so mortal, yet it's exactly what we need to do.

"Aren't you excited, Owen?" Ophelia giggles. She actually is giggling.

"Why would he be excited for a date? I get being excited to see her, but a date? Really?" Julian deadpans.

"Because it's romantic." She sighs, practically glowing. "That's it. You're taking me on a date, Julian Duvain."

"Joys of having a mate," he mutters under his breath.

"Did you say something?" Ophelia arches a brow.

"Nothing, Little Artist," he says smoothly. "Nothing at all."

I let out a boisterous laugh. "Can't say I'm not looking forward to this."

I leave them bickering. I think I hear my name tossed in once. Maybe twice. But there's no way I'm stepping into an argument between those two. I like living.

I portal straight to Bella's apartment. Well the hallway anyway. I put feelers out to make sure no one would be walking around. I don't need to explain my sudden appearance out of thin air to anyone, it sounds like a nightmare.

I take a deep breath before knocking on her door.

When she opens it, it hits me all over again—how goddamn beautiful she is. Not just her face, but the way she looks at me like I'm not a monster.

Her dress hugs her like it was made for this moment, the soft sapphire fabric making her green eyes even brighter against her sun-kissed skin. Dark brown waves fall loose around her shoulders, catching the light with every small movement. But it's the way she smiles—like I'm the only one who gets to see her like this—that completely wrecks me.

"Hey, you," she says, smiling like it's just us in the world.

"You look... breathtaking." The words catch in my throat before I can stop them.

She tilts her head, that smile growing. "You're not so bad yourself."

I offer my arm. "Ready for our very mortal, very proper date night?"

She loops her arm through mine, close enough that I feel the heat of her skin. "As long as there's food involved."

I chuckle. "Alright. Priorities are noted. Let's get to the restaurant before you change your mind."

The restaurant is one that Ophelia recommended—tucked between two art galleries, all low lighting and soft music that hums like a heartbeat. Gold accents catch the candlelight and the smell of roasted garlic drifts in the air. It's intimate without being stuffy. Romantic without trying too hard.

Bella glances around, eyes lighting with curiosity. "Okay, this is gorgeous."

I pull out her chair. "Only the best. Thank your sister."

We skim the menu, trading a few light jokes—something about overpriced appetizers and whether demons tip. She tosses out a line about eternal damnation service fees, and I let out a low laugh.

After we order, I glance at her.

She's not looking my way, but I feel her. Still human in all the ways that matter. And yet, undeniably more.

My soulmate.

"I've been wanting this," I say, looking into her emerald eyes. "Not the date, but just time with you. There's no one else. No bad news or anyone trying to ruin our night. No Rhys."

"Me too," she responds with a tilt of her lips. "It feels unreal. Like we blinked and everything changed."

"It feels like it was meant to be, though," I chuckle. "I guess it kind of was. I told myself I never wanted a soulmate, but now... I can't picture life without one."

I don't want to ask her about the divorce. It's been a week since she filed for legal separation. Julia has been taking care of everything. Bella doesn't need to worry about it, but I'm worried about her.

"The legal separation went through," she states matter of factly, surprising me in the process.

"How did you know that's what I was thinking?"

"Owen... you do know I can hear and feel what you're thinking right? Ophelia taught me what to look for, but you don't close yourself off," she says.

"I used to be able to. Maybe not with you," I say.

It's the closest I've come to admitting what she already feels. How open she makes me without trying. How raw.

With others, I can shield. I've trained for it. Lived it. But with her, it's like trying to build a wall out of paper. Completely and utterly useless.

She sees through me. She *feels* me.

I've been alone in my head for centuries. Now she's in here, whether I'm ready or not.

"Rhys is fighting the divorce process." That's like a bucket of ice water dumped all over me. "He claims that I'm rushing into it and we didn't get the chance to talk about it fully. And that I'm moving on before we can come to terms with everything."

"What did Julia do?" I ask.

"She filed a formal response," Bella says, her voice crisp. "Didn't hold back. She laid it all out—timeline of the manipulation, the affair, financial interference, everything. She made it clear he's not just stalling, he's actively trying to punish me for leaving."

I swirl the drink in my hand. "Did Rhys respond?"

"He tried to. Filed a counterclaim full of emotional appeals. Said I was being influenced, that I wasn't thinking clearly, that I was retaliating."

"Classic," I scoff.

"He asked for mediation. Julia shut it down before I even had to say a word. Told the court he had every opportunity to come clean and didn't. This isn't a misunderstanding. It's a consequence."

I reach across the table, just brushing her hand. "You're not letting him rewrite the story, and he's pissed about it."

"Alright, demon man. Let's change the subject," she smiles at me again and my world goes still, she truly is the only thing that matters, the only thing that's ever mattered.

"To what?" I ask, curiously, tilting my head to the side.

She hums and looks around the room before her eyes light up and she meets my gaze again, I could look at that face forever and never be tired of it. "What's your favorite color?"

That catches me off guard, I shudder for a second before answering. "Wait seriously?"

"I'm always serious." She is laughing so hard she can barely sit straight.

"Charcoal."

The scrunch of her nose makes me laugh along with her. "Charcoal? Like grey?"

"Yeah... why?" I narrow my eyes, a little afraid what she is going to say.

"I was expecting, you know, fire and brimstone. Red. Anything, but grey, that's so...boring." She chuckles.

"What about yours?" I ask her. I want to know. Which is weird. I never cared before.

"Red," she says.

"Ah so *you* love fire and brimstone," I say.

"Okay okay," she continues. "To the most important question."

"Which is?"

"How old are you?"

Well that was unexpected, I don't even know what to say. "How old do I look?" *Really? That's the best I got?*

"At least a couple hundred years old," she says, neutrally. Which is the funniest thing she could've said.

"Close. 301 years old," I say, lifting a brow, anticipating her reaction. That seems to catch her off guard. It was a joke at first, but now it's real.

"You wear it well," she says, eyes narrowing with a smirk. "Not a single wrinkle in sight. That must be amazing. Watching the world change."

"Yeah," I say, smiling just a bit. "I guess. Being immortal does have its perks."

I can hear her phone going off. "Let me put it on vibrate."

She takes it out of her purse and furrows her brow.

"Who is it?" I ask.

"Josie. She's at Hearthlight with the night manager," she says, biting her lips it's a nervous habit I've noticed. "They never call unless it's an emergency."

Call her back," I state firmly.

"Are you sure?" She asks, giving me a questioning glance.

"Positive. You said they wouldn't interrupt unless it's an emergency."

Her phone rings again and this time, she answers. "Hey, Josie. What's —"

Her posture straightens. Whatever she's hearing, it's not good.

"No. I'll be right there." A pause. "Yes. Keep her in the office and lock the back. I'm leaving now."

She ends the call, already standing.

"Tiana's ex-husband showed up," she says quickly. "Violent history. She came to us a few weeks ago for help—got her a rush divorce. He wasn't supposed to know where she was."

I toss a few bills on the table and. stand. "I'm coming with you."

The portal snaps open with a ripple of light as soon as we're in a secluded alley, and we're inside Heartlight before the sound finishes fading. I follow Bella's lead, this is her world.

"What's wrong?" She looks frantic. I've never seen her like this before.

"He's here," Josie responds, looking flushed.

"Who is this man?" I ask. I'm not going to let Bella get into trouble. Not on my watch.

"Derek Holloway. Tiana's husband," Josie says, looking at me.

"Josie. This is Owen. Owen, Josie." Bella may be introducing us, but clearly, it is not what's on her mind. "Have the police been called?" She continues on.

"Yes, but they aren't here. We have the slowest response times in the city. Thanks to the Creed family and all," Josie scoffs.

"Right," Bella says, turning into work mode. "Time to have a talk with Mr. Holloway. You got the kids and Tiana?"

"Yeah. They're with the assistants in the classroom. I didn't want them in the playroom just in case there's arguing."

"Okay. Let's go," she says, steeling herself. But I'm not about to let her just walk out there with someone who is potentially violent.

I walk over to the door and stand in front of it before they could leave. "I don't think so."

"Owen, move. I have something to take care of," Bella says, jaw tight, eyes narrowed. Her anger isn't pointed at me, she's just done waiting.

"I know you're irritated. You don't have a plan though. You're going in blind without knowing who Derek is."

"It doesn't matter who he is," Bella shouts, throwing her hands into the air. "He can't just waltz in here and—"

"I get that, Belladonna. I do, but they have him in the lobby right? Security controlled him?"

"Yes, they did." Josie answers.

"So it's time to find out who he is, make a plan, confront him," I say.

"Fine, what do you want to do?" *God, I love her stubborn side.*

Owen: *Anyone available. I need all the information you can find on Derek Holloway.*

"Did you just do what I think you did?" Bella raises a brow at me.

"Yup," I chuckle.

"Josie, I need you to stay with the kids," she turns to the other woman.

"Got it. For what it's worth... I like him," Josie says, smirking at me.

I laugh, but sober up quickly when the information starts coming in.

It's not good. He was a cop. *Fucking hell*. A cop that has a major drinking problem. My cousins and brothers dug up that he resigned. It doesn't sound like he was going to be fired anyway. There is a pattern of her calling the police and running away, but she always calls him and wants to go back.

"Is there a possibility that she called him to come back and get her?" I ask Bella.

"No. She wouldn't. She's made leaps and bounds. Plus she didn't have a phone. until..." she says, defensively before trailing off.

"When did she get a phone, Belladonna?"

"Today, but she wouldn't..." Bella trails off. The look on her face changes everything. "Emery!" She shouts.

A second later a young girl comes into the office. Bella's assistant, I'm assuming.

"I need you to get Tiana's phone from her. Now!"

She turns and leaves without a word and comes back holding a phone.

"She wouldn't give it to me. She also looked guilty when I took it from her, forcibly I might add," Emery stated in the most monotone voice I've ever heard.

Clearly, they are both trying to keep their emotions in check. Bella looks through the phone and I'm waiting on pins and needles.

"Damnit!" She screams. "She called a number six times in the last twelve hours."

"We don't know for sure it's him," Emery says.

"One way to find out," Bella says. She takes the phone and walks out of her office. I follow close behind. I can hear screaming all the way down the hall.

"Let me go you fucking bastards! Don't you know who I am?!" Derek, I'm assuming, spits out.

We round the corner and I see him. He's tall and put together. Dark hair slicked back, polo shirt, and khakis. Red faced and angry.

Bella pulls out the phone and calls the number. One ring. Two. Across the room, Derek's phone buzzes.

He answers without checking the screen. "Hello?"

"Busted," Bella says, her voice ice.

His face crumples into something ugly.

"Are you fucking kidding me?" he shouts, storming toward us with unsteady steps, breath reeking of booze and bitterness. He gets in Bella's face, spit flying. "You little bitch—"

I step in front of her so fast I barely remember moving.

"Nope," I say, voice low, planting myself between them. "This is not happening. Back the fuck up."

He jabs a finger toward my chest, rage burning behind bloodshot eyes. "Who's going to make me? You?"

His breath hits me—sour, rotten, laced with desperation.

"I wouldn't try if I were you," I whisper.

He laughs, short and harsh. "Fucking try me, asshole."

That's all I need. I strike before he can even see what's happening. I knock his ankle just enough to shift his balance, then slam him against the wall with one hand around his throat.

My voice drops, darker now, layered with the power I'd been given. "See, I gave you a warning."

"Owen. No," Bella says behind me, calm but firm—her voice cutting through the haze.

"Tiana is mine. Always has been, always will be. I just need to remind her what being with me means," Derek snarls.

My grip tightens without meaning to. He doesn't stop. "That bitch director keeps sticking her nose in where it doesn't belong. She won't last long. I know people. Ones who want her gone and can make it happen. Women like her? They disappear."

He smiles in a way that I think was supposed to be intimidating, but the haze in his eyes dulled the effect.

"It's just a matter of time before she will too."

I lean in close, my voice is pure venom. "You just confessed to threatening a woman in front of witnesses."

"Police! Open up!"

His eyes go wide.

Two officers step in. They hesitate for a second. Probably because he was one of their own for a while. Good thing they think better of just letting him go. Derek's arms are pinned behind his back, and he's shoved toward the hallway, still yelling about rights and lies and how this isn't over.

"We need to handle Tiana," Bella sighs, rubbing the bridge of her nose.

"How do you want to do that?" I ask.

Literally out of nowhere, Emery appears. "We could call CPS. We may need to. She's a danger to those kids."

"I agree," Bella says. "Call them. Send Tiana to my office. I need to have a chat with her."

"Are you okay, sweetheart?" I ask on our way back to her office.

"I just had so much hope for her, but she called him. I know that it's normal, this type of stuff happens, it comes with this line of work. But it still sucks."

"You want it for them more than they want it themselves," I say.

"Yeah. Sometimes. It's part of the job." She looks so bone tired. I wish I could take all of this off her shoulders.

Tiana steps into the doorway, uncertain but composed.

Her hands are clasped in front of her, fingers twisting gently, nervous. Shame tugging at her shoulders, but strength holding her upright. "You wanted to see me?"

Once she is in, I close the door behind her. I'm not going to let her be alone with Bella. Not now or ever.

"Yes. You put all of the lives of the women here in danger by calling Derek... six times!" Bella fights hard to keep her voice down. "I'm having Emery put in a call to CPS."

"You're going to take my children from me?!" She yells.

"I should've made the call weeks ago. But I wanted to give you the benefit of the doubt." I've never seen her eyes this hard, if I'm being honest, it's pretty hot.

"What the hell?!" She paces back and forth.

"I believe you both are unfit parents and my recommendation is to remove the children from your care until you seek proper mental health care," Bella says in a way that leaves no room for argument. That is it.

She sits at her desk with Tiana's file and opens it to sign something. My eyes are on Tiana. She picks up a vase and I move, reacting without thinking.

I move, cutting between her and Bella just as she swings.

The vase shatters against the back of my head. A bit of pain rings my ears as the shards scatter across the floor.

Bella gasps.

Tiana freezes, her eyes wide, breath hitching like she didn't quite know what just happened.

"I—" she stammers. "I didn't—"

I straighten slowly, turning toward her. Blood's already trickling down my neck.

Her face crumples. She wasn't aiming for me. She was aiming for Bella.

"Owen! Are you okay?" Bella scrambles to check for a wound. But she won't find one, it's already healed.

I turn and let my eyes swirl from gold to red. It doesn't hurt or burn. It feels like second nature. Time for hell to play.

I walk straight to Tiana, grab her shoulders, and stare into her eyes. She looks at me with wide, terrified eyes as my face transforms.

See that's the thing with being a demon. I can transform into your worst nightmare. The biggest monster you've ever seen. Although it's different for everyone. Their fears are personal. I control them, but don't create them

Tiana screams at the top of her lungs and Derek comes pounding through the door.

"I thought you were arrested," Bella says incredulously.

"They let me go. Helps to know who the arresting officers are... and the DA," Derek says with a smirk, still swaying slightly from the drinks he's consumed.

"Good. Now you can go to Hell," I say, turning to him, a manic smile stretching across my face.

I let all the power I possess take over and see a portal open up beneath his feet. His mouth opens, but no sound comes out as he falls.

"Derek!" She screams before whirling on me, more anger shows on her face than when her children's lives were in danger. "What did you do?!" Tiana screams.

"The only reason you're not going with him is your kids. They need you. So shape up or you'll end up just like him."

She runs out of the room and I hear Bella gasp. I look at her, but she's looking in the picture window to the playroom. Right at Josie, who saw everything. She looks horrified, and Bella looks devastated.

"I need to talk to her. Tell her everything," she stutters out.

"Are you sure?"

"She's my friend," she says. I know she made up her mind.

Well shit. Here we go.

Chapter Seven

Arabella

Josie witnessed everything. Owen's demon brand of justice, Tiana's fear, and Derek disappearing. This is probably the worst case scenario next to the police seeing it.

"I need to talk to her. Tell her everything," I mutter out.

"Are you sure?" Owen asks earnestly.

"She's my friend," I say, looking directly at him. "I can't just not explain."

I run straight into the playroom next door and I find her on the phone.

"Yes. We need police at the Hearthlight Center. I saw—"

I grab the phone from her. "My name is Arabella Arden. I am the owner and director of Hearthlight Center. We will not need your assistance. I'm sorry it was a false alarm. We have it all under control"

"Thank you, ma'am," the operator says. "We just dispatched people to your location not too long ago."

"They arrived, but the situation is under control now. We're safe. Do you have an ETA on when CPS is arriving?"

"They are en route with the police," she says.

"Thank you," I reply, hanging up.

"What the hell?" Josie says, taking her phone back. Her eyes are wide with panic and fear. "You're out of your damn mind—"

I understand what she must be feeling right now, what she just witnessed is not something that our minds are equipped to handle out of nowhere. To make it worse, it's coming on the heels of a woman who just went back to her husband after an incredibly traumatic incident, not just for her, but for all of us.

"Josie!" I whisper-shout, not wanting to alarm the kids, while trying to snap her out of her panicked spiral. We need to talk," I say, reaching for her hands, looking for anyway to ground her.

She jerks away, eyes wide. "Don't touch me! You—he—what is this?" She backs into the corner, panic radiating off her in waves.

"Listen to me, Josie. You know me, you care for the kids in this room, please calm down so we can explain. You know the kids will start panicking," Locking eyes with her and keeping my breathing even, I want her to mimic me. "I need you to calm down, please."

Owen's there, watching with a steady, calming presence. She's staring at him with pure terror in her eyes. Like her worst nightmare just crawled out of the floorboards.

"Owen is a demon." I decide to just go with it now that I said it. "And he's my soulmate."

"Subtle, babe." Owen barks out a laugh.

"I panicked," I mutter, shooting him a scowl.

"A demon? Like fallen angels and evil from Hell demons?" Josie stammers out.

"Not evil," I jump in. "Complicated, but not evil."

"You don't have to explain," Owen tries to cut in. "She's just scared, love."

"She is scared, which is why I need to explain. It might help her get a grasp on what she just saw." I turn my attention back to her gaze, holding it once again. "She's one of my best friends. She deserves to know the truth. Especially with everything she has seen."

I tug down my collar and show her my mark. "This burned into me the day we saw each other for the first time. Think of it like magic, Josie. Babe, show her yours."

Owen pulls up his sleeve and shows her his. "Same here."

"You can't be serious! You're insane!" Josie shouts. "This is just—this is absolutely insane. It's not real!"

"I know. I understand. I was the same way when Ophelia was marked," I say. "Listen, sweetie, I need you to keep your voice down, thinking about the kids playing in the corner, they've seen enough chaos. Just breathe with me."

"Ophelia? Your sister? That means Julian is a— demon." Now she is shaking, but her voice is lower, she's calming down.

I want to reach out to Ophelia. Maybe if she hears from both of us, she'll understand.

Owen: *Just ask her.*

Okay. Here goes nothing.

Arabella: *I need some help, Ophelia. Josie saw Owen. She knows everything and she is struggling. Can you help me?*

Ophelia: *I'll be there in a second. Need Julian to come too?*

Arabella: *Might be best if he stays home. Subtly is not his specialty.*

She really did come through because not even a minute later, a portal appears in my office and two people come walking out.

"I told you not to bring Julian," I sigh.

"He asked where I was going, Bella. I couldn't lie. This is his twin and soulmate that are involved," she says.

"Fine. But please try to be nice, Julian. As in not your blunt usual self," I say, looking directly in his eyes.

"Josie, I know this sounds like complete insanity. I thought the same thing once. But this?" Ophelia gestures to the faint swirling of the portal that's starting to disappear. "It's real. The demons, the magic, soulmates. It's all real. The world is bigger than you could've ever imagined before."

"I'm not sentimental, but my Little Artist is telling the truth," Julian says.

Ophelia smiles softly at her soulmate. "You don't have to believe it all tonight. But you can believe this—Bella would never lie to you, Josie. Owen would never hurt her. You don't have to fear them. They're only after those who call and make deals. The ones that deserve it."

"We didn't choose this," I say. "But we love it anyway."

Josie's voice is barely a whisper. "And if I don't believe in any of it?"

Ophelia meets her gaze. "Then you'll have no reason to speak to anyone about it."

"So demons are real," Josie mutters. "Next you'll tell me the Tooth Fairy is your upstairs neighbor."

"No, but she used to date a vampire." I point at Ophelia.

Julian's eyes flash crimson for a beat. "You've only seen the door open. You haven't met what's on the other side."

"Way to be ominous," Owen snorts.

"Why don't we all go home? Let this settle a bit." Ophelia turns and gives me a huge hug. "Josie here needs a bit to process everything before we get into the specifics."

"Everything will be okay, sis. She'll understand. I weaved this," she whispers in my ear.

"That's another problem I have." Josie starts pacing. "I lost my apartment."

"You what!" I exclaim before shooting a glance at the children in the corner and lowering my voice. "When?"

"Two weeks ago," she says. "I just couldn't keep it. It was in a Creed building."

"You never said a word," I say quietly.

"I didn't want to worry you," she says.

"You can stay with me. At my place."

"Really? You're okay with that?" She asks.

"Of course! Plus it gives us some time to talk."

"Why don't you stay with Owen, Bella?" Ophelia says.

"No. Josie and I need to talk. Maybe I can stay tomorrow?" I look straight at Owen.

"Yeah," he says, kissing my cheek. But I see the way his face drops for a second, he was excited. "I'll see you tomorrow."

And just like that, he's gone along with Julian and Ophelia, vanishing into that soft snap of space tearing itself open and stitching shut behind them.

Josie exhales next to me. "He really just—okay. Cool. Normal Tuesday."

I grab my keys and head toward the hallway. "Wine?"

"You read my damn mind."

We don't say much on the short walk to my place. Inside my apartment, I head straight to the cabinet, grabbing two glasses and the bottle that's been waiting for a night like this.

Josie plops onto my couch and groans. "Demons? Really, Bells?"

"Yeah," I fidget with my fingers, smiling slightly. "It's not like I made the choice. But Josie, I wouldn't have it any other way."

"At least he's better than Rhys," she says, taking a sip.

"Better? What do you mean?"

"I didn't want to tell you, but I *know* he is an asshole," she says.

"You never said anything."

"You were in love. Or obsessed. Whatever. I wasn't gonna be the bad guy." She smirks, but she narrows her eyes. "Okay, spill. What's the actual deal with Owen? Because soulmates? Sounds unreal."

"It happened at Ophelia's Infernal Union," I reminisce back to that moment.

"Infernal Union?" She asks, brows furrowed.

"Wedding, but Hell's way. We were at the party after and Rhys convinced me to tell Ophelia we got married," I say.

"Convinced you... shocker." They way her eyes roll and she takes a sip of wine tells me exactly how she feels about him.

"Anyway the mark seared into me." I shift, pulling my knees up to my chest. "It was physically brutal. Eventually it became more like a scar. But I felt it. When I looked at him. It was like something branded me from the inside out. I wanted to throw up and cry and scream all at once. My whole body was shaking."

Josie sets her wine down and moves closer. No teasing, no jokes. Just her, steady and warm. "Why didn't you tell me?"

"I couldn't make sense of it. It felt too big. Too real." I blow out a breath, look to the sky, and admit the truth. "And I didn't want it to be true."

"But it *is*," she says gently.

I nod, my throat thick. "Yeah. He's my soulmate. And I hate how that sounds. Like I'm in some twisted fairy tale. Like I'm just... supposed to accept this thing that changed my whole existence."

"Well clearly you accepted it." She squeezes my hand tighter.

"I will never regret it either. Owen is everything I've ever dreamed of and more. He didn't get upset about our date being cancelled. He came with me and took care of the problem."

"And you liked that," she says, figuring me out right away. "Someone taking care of you without an agenda."

I look away. She's right and I'm not uncomfortable with it. I like it. I guess on some subconscious level, I always knew Rhys was using me. What I want now is this whole thing with Rhys over so I can move on.

Sensing my desire to change the subject, Josie takes charge. "I want to know about demons. What do they do?"

I blink. "You mean, like, job description? Or extracurriculars?"

She shrugs. "Both. I need a demon crash course. Are they all hot? Do they eat people? Is Owen going to sprout wings and drag you to Hell?"

I laugh, for real this time. "No wings. Not that I've seen. And they don't eat people. At least not the ones I've met."

"That's not exactly comforting." Josie narrows her eyes.

"They're complicated," I say, swirling the wine in my glass. "Made of old magic. Bound to rules. Some serve Powers. Some don't. They trade in contracts, power, emotion..."

"So, demons are like... what, fallen angels? Cursed humans?"

"Neither," I say. "They're born. Like us. Children of old magic. They can conceive, carry, create."

Josie blinks. "Wait, like... actual biological kids?"

I nod. "Yes. They're not made. They're born. Owen was *born*."

"That's... a whole new category of terrifying."

"Yeah. But it also makes them real. They feel, bleed, love. They just live longer. A lot longer. Immortally long." I smile faintly.

Josie processes that. Stunned silence is not something I'm used to with her.

"Like, *forever* immortal?"

"Since the bond formed. Since fate stepped in and rewrote everything I thought I understood about myself."

She lets out a breath. "So you're immortal and soul bound to a demon who can have kids and can portal in and out of the underworld."

"I'm not sure about the immortal thing, now that I think about it. I assume so? I mean Owen's aunt and mom are immortal. Maybe we are too." I make a mental note to ask about that.

"Jesus. Your love life just went mythic."

"Tell me about it." I laugh, but it doesn't quite reach my eyes.

We chat for the entire night. Not sleeping. What's another all nighter in my life? It's nice that Josie knows, though. I can talk to someone other than my sister and Della about all of this now, she's definitely still uncomfortable with it, but she's not running.

That's a start.

Chapter Eight
Arabella

I hear it before I see it. A whooshing sound. Here comes a portal.

What I'm learning now is that everyone's magic leaves a signature, and portals are no exception. They're personal. Reflective. Like fingerprints made of power.

Brushstrokes bloom across the room in soft charcoal and smoky grey washes. The lines are still fluid, still breathtaking. Her touch is as graceful as ever. Even though it's drained of color, it's art.

Ophelia walks through with Owen and Julian.

Her eyes scan the room. She looks calm. Not panicking. That seems like a good sign. "How did she take it?"

Before I can answer, the office door creaks open behind them.

Josie slips in, still in her work clothes, hair pulled back, a tired but stubborn glint in her eyes. She's holding a cup of tea. Probably her third by now.

"I'm not locking myself in a fallout shelter, if that's what you're worried about," she says, laughing slightly.

Julian turns to her, surprised but amused. "You're holding it together quite well."

"I cried last night. I googled weird things. Maybe stress cleaned Bella's kitchen. But I'm fine." She crosses the room and perches on the arm of the couch near me. "I do want to know more, though. About demons. Fate. Whatever this bond thing is. Not tonight. It's been a long day."

"Why? What happened today?" I ask, I hadn't heard about anything from the office. There's a slight panic in my voice.

"Malakai wouldn't sit through story time. Threw his chair, started screaming about how he didn't want to be here if his mom couldn't be."

"He said that?" My chest tightens. It's normal for kids to feel this way, even about the ones who were abusive sometimes. None of us truly know what they've witnessed, oftentimes their non abusive parent is one of the only things that makes them feel safe in life, and this is a new environment, new people, new life for the poor things.

"Word for word." She sighed and looked at the ceiling.

Ophelia tilts her head. "Who's Malakai?"

"He's Tiana and Derek's son," I say quietly.

Ophelia's brow furrows. "Wait—Derek. The guy Owen sent to Hell?"

Josie looks over, confused. "That's what happened?"

Owen nods once. "Yeah. Derek was... not a good man."

"To say the least," I say. "Now Malakai and his little brother are in emergency care, and they don't understand why their mom isn't allowed to take them home."

Josie speaks up again, her voice gentler now. "He's three. He doesn't have the language for any of this. Just feelings and fear. And he doesn't know where to put them."

Ophelia swears under her breath.

"I just sat with him," Josie says. "Let him cry until he wore himself out."

I squeeze her hand. "You did good."

Josie yawns. "Anyway. I'm useless tonight. I need a shower and zero questions."

"What do you think, Belladonna? Want to see my place?" The huge smile on his face reminds me of a kid in a candy shop.

I don't need to say anything because my look says it all. I want to see his place.

"Here's the keys." I hand them over with a smile. "I'll see you tomorrow?"

"Yeah." She smiles at me and pulls me in for a hug. "I hope to get to know more of you, Owen. Please take care of her, she takes care of everyone all the time, she needs a break."

"Sounds good," he says, giving her a wry laugh.

I look at Owen. Really look at him. He's concentrating on something. Julian is staring at him too, but he's trying to cover his laugh.

Ophelia summons a portal and the four of us walk through it, leaving a very in awe Josie in the living room.

"Well this is our stop," Ophelia says, as we walk out to her house. "Owen's house is on the other side of the garden."

"Garden?" I ask.

"Yeah," she says, a smile, prideful smile on her face. "I made it."

"Why am I not surprised," I tisk, grinning at the foliage all around me.

"Enjoy your night you two! Don't do anything I wouldn't do!" She says, winking as she and Julian walk hand in hand inside.

We walk in the opposite direction through Ophelia's garden. It's the first time I've seen it—and it's nothing like I expected.

Owen's place is nestled behind ivy draped stone walls, a mix of old world charm and modern restraint. The door opens into high ceilings, moody wood floors, and shelves filled with books that look like he's actually read them. Everything feels intentional—dark tones, clean lines, soft light filtering in from high windows.

But interestingly enough, there is some bright color to it. A pale pink throw drapes over the couch with matching pillows piled in the corners. They seem almost off. Like they aren't his to begin with. Owen doesn't seem like the... pink type.

"Uhhhh pink pillows?" I ask, picking one up with a raised eyebrow. "They're soft."

"Seth! Caleb!" Owen bellows, storming around the room with a flush of embarrassment creeping up his neck. Honestly, watching it is one of the cutest things I've ever seen. Who knew a demon blushing would turn someone on so much?

"Why are you calling them?" I laugh.

"Because I asked them to make sure the place is clean, not to conjure every pink decoration in the mortal world!"

"Well, I think it's quite—" I'm cut off by two men popping up in front of him.

"You called?" Seth smirks.

"Really?" Owen grunts.

"You said to come and make sure everything was clean. We did that." Caleb walks straight to me and envelops me in a huge hug.

"I did the bedroom. The best one," Seth says, winking at me.

"Do not look at her like that or do that!" Owen exclaims, eyes wide.

"We're off. Have fun, cuz!" Caleb says, laughing.

They disappear into Seth's portal that I swear sparkles like a young girl's dream.

"They were the only ones available," Owen says. "I wanted to make sure that the house was perfect for you."

"Where do they live?" I ask. "Does everyone live on this property?"

"No." Owen takes my hand and tucks it protectively in his arm. "Seth and Caleb live in the middle of the city in an apartment building. Lucas lives out in the Hell fields. Damian and Adrian both are deal makers, but also punish souls. They live in a shared room next to the entrance of the damnation hall."

"So why here?" I ask.

"I don't know. To be close to my family I guess," he says.

"You are a softy," I tease.

He rolls his gold eyes and pulls me in to kiss me. "How about we finish our date?"

I arch a brow. "Here? What happened to candlelight and dessert?"

Owen lifts a hand, fingers snapping once. In a blink, a bottle of deep red wine and two elegant glasses appear on the coffee table—alongside a rich chocolate tart with sugared berries.

"Candlelight and dessert," he echoes, smug.

I can't help the laugh that bubbles out. "Okay, that's cheating."

He leans in, whispering in my ear. "Demon perks."

Once I'm settled on the couch, holding one of the powder pink pillows, he pours me a glass of wine, brushing his fingers to mine as he hands it to me. The contact is just long enough to make my skin tingle.

"Back to the question game. What do you do for fun? I swear if you say strike fear in mortals, I will smack you," I laugh out.

"There goes my first answer," he says, snapping his fingers and grinning at me.

I nudge his shoulder. "Seriously."

He thinks for a moment, swirling the wine in his glass. "I like deals. Figuring out what someone really wants—and whether they deserve it. Collecting information, dirt on people, it really helps to know exactly what makes them tick."

"That's not a hobby, that is your job" I say, raising a brow.

"It's a hobby when you're a demon," he shoots back with a smirk. "But fine. I read. A lot."

"Really?" I curl my legs beneath me on the couch and glance at him. "Okay, real talk—what's your favorite genre?"

He gives me a look, he's trying to play dumb. "Genre of what?"

"Books. You said you read. Don't dodge this."

He sighs dramatically, setting his wine down. "Fine. But if you mock me, I'm revoking your dessert privileges."

I make a zipper motion over my lips.

He leans in slightly, like he's sharing a secret. "Romance."

I blink. "Seriously?"

"There's something about it," he says with a shrug. But the softness in his eyes gives him away. "The tension. The hope. The way people fight like hell to be with each other, even when everything's stacked against them."

"You're a secret romantic," I murmur.

"I'm more Heathcliff than Mr. Rochester." He lets that sink in.

"What's your favorite book?" I breathe.

"*Wuthering Heights*."

"Really?"

He lets his fingers brush mine. "It's about a man who loved someone so much he made his own soul darker. He returned like a storm to claim what was his—even after it destroyed everything around him."

Something in my chest tugs. *God help me, I'm already falling.*

His vulnerability is intoxicating. I can't help myself.

I lean in, and for a heartbeat, nothing else exists except the soft curve of his lips against mine. When he presses back, gentle and searching at first, I don't pull away. My fingers slip into his hair, tugging just enough to draw a low, slow inhale from him. It makes something burned over in me come back to life.

He smiles into the kiss before his lips find mine again. It's deeper this time, more urgent. I slide higher onto his lap, pressing my hips into his thighs. The couch shifts under us so I can rest my arms around his shoulders, pulling him impossibly closer.

Something stirs in my chest—something that smells of promise and danger. This isn't just lust. It's more than that. It's a longing like I've been waiting my entire life for this moment, for him.

He murmurs into my mouth. I feel it more than hear it. "You undo me."

His hands tighten across the small of my back like he's pleading to hold me in place before he loses control. I bite my bottom lip, tasting him on it. The heat of his breath, the hardness of his body pressed to mine, it all pulses through me in waves.

I shift again, draping a leg over his. Our thighs part and press together as I lean into every inch of contact. My heart hammers both because of what we're doing and because of who he is—the ferocity of him. The power that barely tames itself for my sake. He is all tension and strength and river deep emotion, and somehow he fits around me like home.

His fingers find the hem of my shirt. Slowly he lifts it bit by bit, dragging it up like he's leading me deeper into something I hadn't known I needed. My bra is gone in a blink. His breath hitches over the sweep of my collarbone. His mouth follows the line of my neck, slow and wet, and I gasp.

I don't even think about shutting the moment down. I let him explore me. This isn't about losing myself. It's about choosing to give it. Pieces at a time.

My head tilts back when he kisses across my collarbone down to my mark. His hand curves into the dip of my waist unconsciously. His thigh braces under me like he's holding on to keep from falling. My blood thrums around the heat of his. He tastes my skin on his tongue as he kisses above my breast.

We're partners. He wants me. And above everything, I want to be worthy of him in this kind of giving.

He breaks the kiss finally, breath ragged. His forehead presses to mine. I can feel his breath and his pulse slamming under my palm. I rest my chest against him, dizzy in the collapse of emotion and desire.

I want him. More than I've wanted anyone ever.

"I should stop," he says against my lips. "I should wait until you're divorced," he adds. "I'm not going to cross that line with you like this."

I close my eyes for a second. As disappointed as I am, I know where he's coming from. I really do.

When I look at him again, I nod. "You're right," I say, my voice soft but sure. "As much as I want this—us—I don't want anything about it to be tangled in him."

"I want you so badly it physically hurts," he says, resting his forehead against mine. "But I'm not touching you like that until you're free. Fully."

"You're kind of infuriatingly perfect, you know that?" I brush my nose against his.

"Don't say that," he groans.

We both laugh, and it breaks the tension just enough to let go of some of the indignation.

He kisses my forehead again, lingering there like he's imprinting the moment.

"Come on," he murmurs. "Let's get some rest."

We get up slowly, holding hands, reluctant to let the moment end. He laces his fingers with mine and leads me toward the bedroom.

His room is nothing like I expected.

The walls are painted charcoal, but there are fairy lights strung across the headboard. Candles flicker on the dresser in aesthetically curated clusters. A fluffy white throw is draped across the foot of the bed, which is layered in soft, jewel toned bedding. There's even a rose in a glass vase on the nightstand.

I turn to look at Owen, trying not to laugh.

"Damnit, Seth."

That does it—I crack up, a full laugh bursting out of me. "Oh, he really went for it."

"He said he was just making it less bachelor pad, not staging a proposal like those damn mortal dating reality shows." Owen rubs the back of his neck, half embarrassed, half amused.

I walk further into the room, brushing my fingers over the velvet pillow sham. "Honestly? I kind of love it."

"Then I guess it's all staying." He rolls his eyes, but he's smiling now too.

I pick up the rose, giving it a mock-serious sniff. "Romantic *and* bold. Very on-brand."

He nudges the pillows back, sitting at the edge of the bed. "You still good with staying here?"

"Yeah," I say, toes curling into the soft rug. "Yeah, I am."

I climb in beside him, and he shifts, letting me settle into the space like I've always belonged there. His arm curves around my shoulders, and I tuck myself in close, cheek to his chest. His heart beats under my ear.

"This okay?" he murmurs.

"It's perfect."

He brushes a hand down my spine. "I want to keep you," he whispers. "Tuck you away here and steal your hours—every thought, every glance. Just mine."

The words curl around me like warmth and want.

Sleep comes easily in his arms. I don't feel restless. I feel at home.

Chapter Nine
Arabella

I wake up the next morning—or what counts as morning in Hell—feeling more rested than I have in years. There's something comforting about sleeping in Owen's arms. It feels naughty. Like I shouldn't be doing it.

But also perfect. Almost like I'm meant to be here. Obviously I am. The mark says it all. But it's one thing to accept the mark, and it's entirely another thing to feel it.

His arm is slung over my waist casually. Our legs are tangled beneath the sheets. My skin is brushing against his. We haven't moved from this position all night.

Stretching my legs, there's the feeling of a smooth, soft fabric gliding over my skin. I pull back the covers and see a light pink silk nightgown with lace overlays. I don't remember putting this on last night. Which means Owen probably conjured it.

I snort out a laugh. Men. All the same.

"Why are you awake?" He groans.

"That's what happens when you're well rested," I say. "I'd like to know how I got this nightgown on."

"I thought you'd want to be comfortable." Owen is smiling, but his eyes are still closed.

"We better get up," I sigh. "What time is it on earth?"

Owen rolls over to grab his tablet. After a few clicks, he says, "It's 7AM your time."

"Shit! I have to go!" I throw the blankets off and get up, running to the closet.

That's when I realize I'm not home. I don't have clothes, a bag...anything. Just this silk nightgown, Owen's sheets, and the demon currently taking up most of the bed.

He looks over at me, relaxed, one arm tucked behind his head, the blankets slung low across his hips like it's the most natural thing in the world.

"Check the closet, Belladonna," he says with a lazy grin. "You might find something."

I pause, the nickname tugging at me. "Why do you call me that?"

His smile shifts, something quieter moving behind it. "Because belladonna's beautiful and deadly. It was used to widen pupils, make lips redder, make men fall for something they never saw coming. That's you. Alluring in a way that feels like a trick of the light, dangerous in a way I'd swallow anyway. You're poison dressed as a gift, and I'd take every drop."

I like that. A lot. It catches me off guard—how easy it is to smile around him now. I glance down at my feet, trying not to let it show too much.

Then it hits me—what he said about the closet.

Curious, I cross the room and pull open the door. The moment I do, I stop.

There are clothes. Hangers and hangers of them. Most in shades I gravitate toward—deep jewel tones, sleek neutrals, soft textures that drape in all the right ways. Some are casual. Some are clearly for work. There's even a pair of boots I swear I almost bought last fall.

But on the other shelf... there's lingerie.

Lace. Satin. Mesh. Strappy things that look uncomfortable and barely held together.

I pick up a set and hold it out with two fingers like it might bite me.

"What is *this*?" I call over my shoulder.

Owen doesn't even lift his head. "Damnit, Ophelia. I asked her to conjure your favorites, not add her own."

"Okay, gross. I don't need to think about my sister picking out your fantasy wardrobe." I groan.

I tuck the ridiculous lace thing back into the drawer and reach for something a little more comfortable. I sift past the lingerie graveyard and pull out a fitted blouse and tailored black trousers. Professional enough that I can wear it to work, yet me enough that I won't feel like someone pretending to be a professional. Add boots, a coat. Done.

"Uh—do you have an extra toothbrush?" I awkwardly ask.

Owen smirks. "Top drawer, left side. Yours now."

I roll my eyes and head to the bathroom. A minute later, I'm brushing my teeth at demonic speed, because now I'm running late and kind of flustered.

Owen watches from the bed, head still propped up, eyes trailing every movement like he's memorizing it.

"Busy day?" he asks.

I grab my bag and nod. "Meeting Julia at Hex & Brews for tea. We're finalizing some court paperwork, then the rest of the girls are showing up to hang out. After that, I've got meetings all afternoon and a site walk-through with Josie. She's helping on the outreach campaign."

"Work, tea, girl gang," he says, like he's filing it all away.

"Exactly. What about you? What terrifying things are you doing while I'm negotiating donor contracts and sipping lavender chai?"

He stretches—long, slow, annoyingly perfect. "I have to check on a few soul deals, reinforce some binding circles, and there's a meeting with the infernal council about a minor uprising. Should be quick."

"Just a casual Tuesday."

He grins. "Don't be late to your tea."

"I won't," I say, already moving toward the door.

But before I go, I pause. Look back.

He's still watching me.

And for a second, I want to stay. Just crawl back into that bed, into his arms, and forget the rest of the world exists. I never felt that with Rhys. Not once. But with Owen... it's different.

He's everything.

Everything Rhys never was.

I'm excited to get this divorce finalized—relieved, even. Because now I know what real love feels like. I thought I wanted a wedding, but that wasn't it. Rhys wanted the paper. I wanted the promise.

With Owen, I finally see what forever's supposed to look like.

I portal to Hex & Brews—still weird, but definitely convenient. *At least I never have to deal with traffic again. I chuckle at my own joke.*

When I look down at my watch, I grin. 8AM. Perfect.

The bell over the door rings as I step inside. The place smells like coffee and toasted cinnamon—comfort in scent form.

Julia's already tucked in a corner booth, waving me over like we're just two normal women meeting for tea and not about to finalize a divorce from a man I probably should've banished myself.

"Hey, Bella!" Julia says. "How are you doing?"

"I'm great! Please tell me you have good news," I say, practically begging.

She sighs and sets her tea down. "He still won't sign."

My stomach drops. "Seriously? I'm not asking for anything. No alimony, no split assets, nothing. He makes triple what I do, and I'm walking away clean."

Julia leans. "I think he just doesn't like that you're actually *leaving*. That you're not begging."

I let out a bitter laugh. "I haven't begged in a long time."

"I know." She sighs. "But Rhys doesn't see it that way. And now his attorney's getting slippery too—stalling filings, not returning my calls."

"So we go all in," I say, sitting up straighter. "No more waiting. No more hoping he'll act like a decent human."

Julia gives me a look I've come to recognize. It's her ready for war look. "We file for a contested divorce, argue obstruction, and request court intervention. We'll show he's refusing to cooperate, and if the judge agrees, we move forward without his signature."

"Do it."

"Already started the paperwork." Julia smiles wickedly.

Before I can reply, the beaded curtain in the back swishes open and Della steps out, adjusting her skirt and tucking a tarot card back into the drawer like she's just finished cursing someone.

"Some woman just cried in my back room because her boyfriend's Saturn return is making him emotionally unavailable," she announces. "I told her to stop dating air signs."

She catches sight of us and raises a brow. "What did I miss? Tell me someone's getting hexed."

"Rhys still won't sign," Julia says, "so we're filing contested."

Della beams. "Ugh, I love it when the legal system gets spicy."

She slides into the booth and plops down, her hands cup her chin as she focuses fully on the conversation. She's way too excited for this..

The front door jingles as Josie and Ophelia walk in as if on cue, Josie waving. That looks like a good sign. Maybe she's adjusting far faster than Ophelia and I did..

"You guys come together?" I ask.

"Yeah," Josie says, sliding into the booth. "We portaled. My first portal. It was actually kind of fun!" She whips her head around, eyes wide. "Wait. I said that out loud."

Julia just raises an eyebrow, sipping her tea like this is all completely normal. "It's fine. We know."

Josie blinks. "You *what*?"

Della smirks, reaching for a muffin. "Oh yeah. We're all in the demon loop now."

"How—when—what?"

Julia sets her cup down. "Partner at my firm? Total demon. His soulmate's immortal too. It's a whole thing. Honestly, she's amazing."

Josie's mouth falls open. "You're serious."

Della leans in, wiggling her fingers with a mischievous grin. "I'm basically a witch."

Josie snorts. "*Basically*?"

Della glances around to make sure no one's looking, then flicks her fingers. Her muffin floats half an inch off the plate, does a slow spin, and lands perfectly upright.

Josie's jaw drops.

"Welcome to the weird side, babe," Della says, biting into the muffin and winking.

Josie blinks, still processing the floating muffin. "Okay. So that's real. Good to know."

"Very real," Julia says.

Della waves a hand. "Anyway, we're not talking about demons. We're talking about brunch."

For the next few minutes, it's easy. Normal. Muffins, coffee, light shit talking. Della makes a crack about a client who cried mid aura cleanse. Ophelia pretends not to judge the café's candle placement. Josie jokes about the possibility of accidentally stepping out into someone's shower.

But eventually, Josie leans back with a sigh. "Work's been chaotic. I love my kids, but if I have to post one more blurry photo with ten hashtags, I'm going to scream."

"Oh my god, same," I say. "I swear, if I see another graphic, I might just combust. I didn't sign up for marketing."

Julia raises an eyebrow. "Hire someone."

"HR actually sent over a candidate they love. I'm interviewing her today." I shrug.

"Please let her be sane," Josie says, sipping her drink.

"Don't get me wrong, I'd definitely prefer sane, but I'd settle for competent." I roll my eyes and sigh.

After another hour, I start looking at my watch. The interview is coming up and I want to prepare for it beforehand, it's been a while since we've hired anyone, and we need to make sure they can keep a secret. I can't have anyone come in that might put our families at risk.

"I love you girls, but I have to head out," I say standing up.

"Me too." Julia stands. "I better get to the office."

Josie and I walk side by side back to the office. It's a gorgeous day, and it feels like such a shame to waste it by portaling.

We walk a few more steps in easy silence, until Josie glances over again, her expression softer now.

"How are the kids doing?" I ask, already knowing who I really mean.

She exhales through her nose. "They're holding on. Barely."

"Malakai?"

Josie nods. "Rough morning. He snapped at one of the aides and threw a chair."

My heart clenches and I wince. "Shit. Is he okay?"

"He misses his mother. He's angry, scared, confused. And no one in that foster house knows how to handle a kid like him. He's not bad, Bella. He's just... breaking."

"I know," I say quietly.

"I sat with him after," she continues. "He wouldn't talk, just kept asking if he was ever going back home."

Silence stretches between us for a beat too long.

"He was so protective of her," I whisper. "Of his brother. Even when we didn't know the full story."

"He still is," Josie says. "He just doesn't know what to do with all the rage."

"I'll take a look at it once we hire this social media grant writing wizard," I say, giving her arm a comforting squeeze.

Josie opens the door to the center and we split off. She's heading to her office by the classroom and I'm heading to mine. When I get in, I notice a file on my desk. Emery is the best. Everything is already put together.

I sit down and open it. The resume looks incredible. Strong non-profit background. Experience in crisis PR and social engagement. Spearheaded two major fundraising campaigns that doubled donor contributions in under a year.

I take a look at the name. Tinsley Creed.

A Creed? HR's strongest candidate is from the family who wants to take Hearthlight down? This is ridiculous.

I don't have time to question it because Emery pokes her head in.

"Tinsley Creed is here for the interview."

"Send her in," I say, resigned.

A moment later, the door opens and I pause.

She walks in like she owns wherever she enters, but not in the arrogant way I expected. No flash, no dramatic flair. Just calm, confident steps and a soft smile that doesn't quite reach her eyes.

Her hair is a cascade of soft brown curls, pulled back into a low, neat twist that still lets a few strands fall loose around her face. Her green eyes flick across the room like she's already noting every detail.

She's in a tailored navy dress, structured but not stiff, with a coat draped over one arm and a leather portfolio in her hand. Minimal makeup, delicate gold hoops, simple heels. She looks... polished and relatable at the same time.

Not at all what I expected from a Creed.

"Thank you for coming in," I say, extending my hand.

"Thank you for having me." Her handshake is firm.

We sit. I glance at the portfolio she offers, even though I already memorized her résumé. "Your background is impressive. Why us?"

She doesn't miss a beat. "Because you're the only place doing work that matters. You're doing it well and for the right reasons, not performatively."

"And you know the Creed name might raise... eyebrows?" I want to be straight with her, but saying that her name alone might raise concerns would be a bit much. I'm trying not to judge based on her family. Lord knows if people judged me by who my father was, I definitely would not be in the position I am today.

"I do," she says, not flinching. "That's why I've spent years earning a reputation that's mine. Not theirs."

I study her. "Social media strategist, crisis PR, nonprofit fundraising... you've done a lot."

"I've cleaned up messy reputations. Launched campaigns for children's hospitals. Spent the last six months ghostwriting for a domestic violence foundation CEO who couldn't go public herself."

That gets my attention. "Why couldn't she?"

"She was still living in the shelter. I kept her name out of the press. She runs that foundation now."

I blink. "And you don't list that on your resumé."

"I protect my clients. Even the ones who can't pay me."

Okay, that's strike one against my cynicism.

"What would you do here?" I ask.

She smiles, and it's brighter now, more natural. "Brand cleanup, obviously. You're under fire from three directions—media, board, and donors. We reposition the narrative. Center the stories that matter. Highlight the success. I'd start with community driven posts—let people see the faces you're saving, not the numbers you're fighting."

I don't even realize I'm nodding until she stops talking.

"Plus," she adds, "I throw a mean fundraiser."

I raise an eyebrow. "What do you mean?"

"Masquerade ball."

That actually makes me laugh. "I hate those things."

"We'll make it a good one." She leans forward, eyes alight now with the kind of excitement I used to have before Rhys drained it all out of me.

"I have to ask," I say. "You know your family's been trying to buy this land for years. Stirring things up. Making problems. So why should I trust you? Why should I hire a Creed?"

She doesn't look away.

"Because I've spent my whole adult life *not* being one. I left all of it. No favors. No trust funds. No shortcuts. And if you want proof—look at my bank account, not my last name."

There's something raw in her voice now. Earnest. She seems like she's a little tired.

"I didn't walk into this interview to represent the Creed family. I walked in because I believe in what you do. And I think I can help."

I hold her gaze.

"What do you need from this job, Tinsley?"

"A clean slate," she says. "A place to make something good. And a boss who won't assume I'm my last name."

"You know that we can't pay you that much, right?" It's one of the things that steers people away typically. "Most of our funding goes to the center."

"I know, I'm prepared for that. These people need help, and I want to put my skills to use in a way that's going to make a difference in the world for the better." She doesn't break my eye contact the entire time she speaks.

I breathe in slowly and offer my hand again. "You're hired."

Chapter Ten
Owen

Ah the Infernal Council. Not the people I love to see. At least I think they're people. No one knows what they look like.

I hate it here. I can't imagine how mortals feel when they check in. We send them to Hell, but people like my mother and aunt make sure the souls are checked in and sent to where their torture chambers are.

This may be Hell, but not in the biblical sense. It's not like only the evil or bad souls come here. Every soul is here. They are sent to where they belong based on their lives. The living never know that. They fear death too much to be told.

As a demon, I mostly take care of the evil of the mortal world. That's a choice. My whole family works this way. Damian and Adrian still take deals, but they punish more now. Julian is collecting more now.

There are also reapers. A demon can be a reaper, but it is hard. Evil is easy, They deserve it. Good people who died from disease or an accident? That is painful. When I look at Bella, I can see her doing that.

Her soul is pure. She's an angel. She'd probably love helping those people.

I shake off my thoughts. If I keep thinking about Bella, I'll never get anything done. All I want to do is go up there and steal her away.

My brothers and cousins are standing at the grand entrance of the Infernal Palace. The doors loom behind them—obsidian, three stories tall, carved with demons in agony. The stone pulses faintly, like it's breathing. Or hungry. Hard to tell with Hell.

History's deadliest contracts are held here. The torture agreements of the worst souls that ever walked the earth are filed in the records hall.

The Infernal Council's chamber is just inside. Getting a summon from them is never a good thing. Julian let us all know that we are all on it. So, we must attend the meeting, there's no getting out of it, if we refuse, they'd simply conjure us from wherever we are anyway.

"Why are we here?" I don't have time for pleasantries.

"Well hello to you too, Owen. I'm *great*, thanks for asking!" Seth throws his hands up like he's offended.

"Really?" I deadpan.

"What? I'm your cousin. A little warmth won't kill you."

"Ophelia came home with the summons," Julian continues on.

"That's not how they usually call people?" I'm confused. They send letters or show up in your living room. Not send a fated mate home with a summons to show at a certain time.

"She works with them more than anyone. She said she felt like it was more convenient to do it that way," Julian says. "You know them. Never normal."

I stare at the doors—bone and blackened runes fused like they were grown rather than built. Not the usual theatrics. These lead to the chamber beneath the Infernal Palace—the one no one enters without cause.

Whatever this is, it's not good.

"Let's see what they need," I say.

We step through the doors into an empty chamber.

Of course it's empty. The Council doesn't arrive—they descend. Always with an entrance. Always on their time. Which means we're early. Or being made to wait.

Blue flames flare to life, hot enough to melt reality at the edges. Overkill, but expected. The Council's never met a subtle entrance they liked.

All seven of them are shrouded in their usual black cloaks, faces nothing but void—empty sockets where identity should be. It's not for mystery. It's for control.

No eyes. No tells. No humanity to manipulate.

"You are on time," the Council says, their voice dragging through the chamber like iron over bone. "Difficult, considering two of you are mated."

Julian inclines his head, composed. "We make time for what matters."

Seth's smile is subdued, almost respectful. "Love hasn't delayed us. Yet."

Damian stands still, hands clasped behind his back. "We assumed urgency. Were we wrong?"

"They circle first," Adrian murmurs. "They always do."

Lucas lifts his gaze, but not his posture. "We're listening."

"The Creeds," the Council says, voice low and dissonant. "They've begun spreading the method on how to summon you to get you to make deals."

Seth scoffs. "What, like some demonic DIY blog? Summon your own soul collector in five easy steps?"

No one laughs.

"Cassius told them," the Council continues. "Now others know."

Julian's expression doesn't shift, but the air around him cools. "How many?"

"Enough," comes the reply. "More than we can silence. Less than we can ignore."

I cross my arms. "We told you the Creed's were up to something."

Julian's jaw tightens. "They're selling it, aren't they."

"Yes," the Council replies. "And mortals are paying. Heavily."

"Desperation," I mutter. "That always fetches a high price. If summoning becomes common knowledge—"

"Mortals will panic," Adrian cuts in. "And desperate mortals make messy contracts."

"They already summon us out of fear," Caleb adds. "If they do it out of curiosity? We're screwed."

"The balance must remain intact," the Council says. "Your family must restore control."

"And if we can't?" Seth asks.

"Then we will."

We turn to leave.

But their voice follows. "One more thing."

We still.

"Della Sage."

Julian glances over his shoulder. "What about her?"

"She brought this to us," the Council says. "The Creeds. The consequences. We might not have seen it in time."

"Of course she did," Seth mutters.

Lucas crosses his arms. "How long has she known?"

"She always knows," I say quietly.

The Council doesn't argue. "She is not a threat," they say. "But she is... unnerving."

"She's a friend," Julian says, voice firm.

"She is a resource," the Council corrects. "One we no longer take for granted."

Adrian lowers his gaze. "She's watching, isn't she?"

"Yes," the Council replies. "If she ever stops watching... *that* is when you should worry."

Blue fire snaps toward the ceiling and just like that, the Council is gone. No warning or farewell.

Julian exhales. "We've got bigger fish to fry now. Who knows how many people have the method."

"We can find out," Damian says. "Start with the next idiot who makes a deal. Torture tends to loosen tongues."

"Or," Lucas says mildly, "we ask. Sometimes mortals answer faster when they still have their soul."

Caleb folds his arms. "If we shut down the Creeds, the summoning curiosity dries up. The balance stays intact. Last thing we need is quote unquote good souls selling themselves for humanity's sake. That kind of martyrdom? Catastrophic."

Julian looks at me. "What does the Creed deal look like?"

I call the contract forward, let the ink reshape in my mind. "Standard exchange," I say. "Their collective success in exchange for Tinsley Creed's soul."

Julian's jaw tightens. "Cassius's influence. One soul to buy the others."

Adrian speaks through clenched teeth. "Anyone know Tinsley?"

"No," I say. "But we will."

I call it a day. Well kind of. It's not like we can clock out per se. But we can shut off the calls, unless it's loud enough or meant for one of us specifically.

I walk home instead of portaling. Sometimes the movement helps me think. I see a stall that catches my eye. A spill of flowers, vibrant and wrong in the best way—petals edged in flame, some pulsing faintly like they're alive. Others bloom in reverse, unraveling inward instead of out. They are perfect for Bella.

"How much?" I ask. "Don't overcharge me."

She tilts her head, all silver eyes and a slow, knowing smile. "I would never," she says, with mock offense. But the way she says it—it's like she's seen this moment before.

"Right," I mutter, chuckling.

Her gaze sharpens. "For your fated mate?"

I blink. "Yes."

She nods, like the answer was obvious. Maybe it was. "Then let me make the bouquet," she says, already reaching for blooms that shimmer and wilt at the same time. "She'll need balance. And you... restraint."

I leave the stall with the bouquet in hand, hoping Bella's home.

Home. That's... an interesting thought. *Home. With Bella.*

But when I step inside, I know right away—she's not here.

It doesn't take long, though. The portal opens and in comes Bella. Groaning like the day has been the longest in all of history.

She takes off her jacket and looks at me, holding her flowers.

"Owen? What are those?" She asks.

"Flowers," I say, even if it is obvious. "I saw them in the market and thought they were beautiful. The seer turned them into the perfect bouquet."

"They're beautiful!" She grabs them from my hands and kisses me, throwing her arms around my neck. "Do they need water?"

"No, they'll never die," I say, kissing her back and smiling at the pure joy on her face. If all it takes is some flowers to make her this happy, I'll buy every single one I can get my hands on.

"Probably good for Ophelia's murder garden. She may be an incredible painter, but that girl couldn't keep anything alive."

I laugh. It's easy with her. She's just a ray of sunshine.

"So how was your day?" She asks, putting the bouquet in the perfect vase and spot on the counter.

"Good," I say. "Until the Infernal Council summoned the Duvains."

"What did they want?" She asks, whirling around to face me again.

"They're worried about the Creeds. They're selling summoning spells to others for a high price and it's tipping the balance."

"Of course those assholes are," she sighs. "Except for Tinsley, of course. Wait they know how to summon? How? Have they made a deal?"

"Do you know Tinsley?" I ask. It'd be perfect if she does.

"Don't change the subject, Owen Duvain." She crosses her arms and taps her foot.

I let out a sigh and run my hand through my dark hair. "Cassius told them how."

"My fucking bastard of a father," she spits out. She starts pacing the room. "He's such a piece of shit. I mean, I know he's already in Hell, but I want to bring him back so *I* can take his soul this time," she adds.

I just watch her huff around the room and rant about Cassius. She's not wrong, he is an asshole. Even if he is her father. But there's something about watching her like this, it almost breaks the restraint I have. I want to grab her up, kiss her, and never let go.

"Hang on..." She trails off. "Did the Creeds make a deal?"

"They did," I say. "Political power and money for Tinsley's soul."

"They traded her soul!" She exclaims. "We have to tell her."

"We can't," I say. "She can't know. Fate will find a way, but we can't interfere. How do you know her?"

"She applied to a job at Hearthlight and I hired her," Bella says plopping on the couch.

"Does she know anything about us?" I ask.

"No, but it's not like I asked either."

"Della brought it to the Council's attention. Apparently she works with them often. Maybe we need to ask her," I say.

"Call a family meeting in the garden," Bella says, getting up. "Let's ask her there."

I open the link in my mind, stretch it toward the others, and relay the message from my mate.

We step beneath the arch. Vines curl in greeting, or warning, depending on their mood. Bella's hand brushes one bloom. It purrs under her touch.

I guide her to the stone bench near the twisted myrrh tree, the one with leaves that turn black when someone lies nearby.

After a few minutes Julian arrives with his arm wrapped around Ophelia's shoulders. Damian and Adrian follow closely behind them.

No Seth. No Caleb. No Lucas.

"They got pulled," Julian says without needing to ask. "Deals came in."

I nod. "I figured."

Adrian sits on the fountain's edge. "This is where we talk about Tinsley Creed?"

"Among other things," I say.

Just as the last word leaves my mouth, the light changes. The kind of shift you don't see—you feel.

Della is here.

Not from the path. Not from a portal. Just... here. "You should've called me sooner."

Della doesn't sit. She never does. She walks the edge of the fountain, fingers trailing along the rim like she's coaxing it to speak.

"You've underestimated them," she says simply.

"The Creeds?" Damian asks.

Della nods. "They've been building toward this for years. Everything about them is constructed to look opulent."

Julian frowns. "Until now, they were privileged. Vain. Self important, maybe—but harmless."

"They are never harmless," Della says. "Not when they're hungry. And the Creeds are starving—for power, for legacy, for something they think they're owed."

Adrian leans forward. "How many have made deals?"

"We don't know," I answer.

"Does she know?" Damian asks.

Della stops walking. We all know that he's talking about Tinsley Creed.

"No," she says. "And none of you can tell her."

"Why not?" Julian asks.

"Because she's the only one left who hasn't made a choice yet." Della's voice is even, but her eyes are unreadable. "The others are bound. Chained by their own greed. But Tinsley..."

She looks at me then. Direct.

"She could still go either way." Della straightens. "Watch her closely."

Adrian tilts his head. "Because she's dangerous?"

"Because she doesn't know she is." Della's smile doesn't reach her eyes.

That's the key, isn't it? No one really knows who the Creeds are.

But she knows her family. The same people threatening to take away the one thing my soulmate loves more than anything.

That's not happening.

Not on my watch.

Chapter Eleven
Arabella

I t's been a couple of weeks since Tinsley started. She's amazing, transforming our social media and opening up donations. There's honestly nothing more I could ask for.

She has been a blessing, but the curse her family put on her is weighing heavily on my mind. They sold her soul. I watched Ophelia go through those emotions when Cassius did it to her, it was pure Hell for her, and not the sort our mates live in.

But I can't focus on that too much at the moment. Today, Julia and I are meeting at the courthouse. We are *finally* going in front of a judge. I want today to be the last day I am Arabella Westwood. I want to rid myself of that stupid name. I'd rather have my maiden name, Arden, back. That thought alone makes me shiver with mild disgust.

I swear I hate men.

But, I won't need to keep that name for long. Soon enough I'll be Arabella Duvain. I'll rid every trace of Rhys from my life.

Julia's standing in the lobby. Her hair is smoothed into a ponytail and she's wearing court attire. This is her arena, she looks perfectly confident.

"You ready?" She asks as I approach.

"I'm ready for this to be over with, that's for damn sure," I sigh. "However, definitely not excited to see his face again.."

"I completely understand. Hopefully things will go in our favor and we can end this," she says.

We're the first to arrive in the small courtroom on the second floor. So, we take our seats at the table and review a few documents, whispering under our breath to one another.

Just a few moments later, Rhys and his attorney enter and take their seats as well. I make a point not to look over at him.

We all stand as the judge sits and the clerk walks over with a file. "Case 34219. Westwood versus Westwood. Motion to compel respondent cooperation in dissolution proceedings."

"Good Morning. My name is Judge Riviera. Let's begin with introductions for the record," Judge Riviera says.

"Julia Carter, counsel for the petitioner, Arabella Westwood," Julia says.

"Kendra Sloane, counsel for the respondent, Rhys Westwood," the other lady says.

"Okay, good. Ms. Carter, you may proceed," Judge Riviera says.

"Thank you, Your Honor. My client, Arabella Westwood, filed for divorce four weeks ago. Since that filing, the respondent—Mr. Rhys Westwood—has failed to sign the documents or participate in any next steps. We are seeking court intervention to compel cooperation," Julia says.

Julia is looking down at her notes and files in front of her as Kendra cuts it. "If I may, Your Honor. Mr. Westwood attempted to reach out to Mrs. Westwood to discuss terms. She blocked him."

Julia hands papers to the bailiff to give to the judge. "We issued formal notice on the third of the month, requesting that all communication be directed through legal counsel. That was done for privacy, protection, and the enforcement of boundaries."

"Understood. Please continue," Riviera says, while flipping through all the paperwork.

"We have also submitted documentation detailing Mr. Westwood's misuse of shared finances. Over $10,000 was spent across seven extra-marital affairs during the marriage. Receipts, wire transfers, and hotel statements are included in the filing. My client was unaware of the extent until our forensic review," Julia continues on.

I try not to flinch, but I do lock my fingers together and squeeze. Over $10k? Seven affairs! He's worse than I thought! In my despera-tion to have someone to love me. To sacrifice everything the way Julian did for Ophelia. The marriage that Ophelia and Julian have now. Hell, my greed. Let's call it what it is... I didn't vet like I would. I didn't look into Rhys like I should have! I'm such a fucking fool.

"Despite all of that, Mrs. Westwood is asking for the right to re-tain what she had prior to the marriage—specifically, the Hearthlight building," Julia says, making me realize that she hasn't stopped talking yet.

"We don't dispute the transactions. However, Mr. Westwood as-serts a claim on the Hearthlight property. While it originated from a pre-marital trust, its growth and sustainability were significantly influenced by the marriage. Mr. Westwood's social standing, network access, and indirect support helped the nonprofit gain credibility and access to certain opportunities. That contribution warrants consider-ation," Kendra says.

I freeze. I can't lose Hearthlight. I'm so mad at myself. I put my life and the shelter in jeopardy. I put everything I worked for at risk. I got nothing out of this marriage. I'm starting to doubt my life. The bond. Being a fated mate. If it's even real. Because my life feels like it's about to end.

"Influence does not constitute ownership. Hearthlight received no funding from Mr. Westwood, no administrative or operational support. He is not listed in any grant proposals, donor contracts, or leadership documentation. My client established Hearthlight through a trust before their marriage. It is a registered nonprofit, and its success came from her labor and sacrifice. The idea that his social proximity gives him a stake is legally and ethically unfounded," Julia says.

"And the respondent's intent for the property?" Judge Riviera asks.

"Mr. Westwood has received a purchase offer from the Creed family. He believes the property has commercial potential that should be leveraged, especially if it's no longer serving its original purpose," Kendra responds to the judge.

"That property is still active. Selling it would dismantle a shelter for women. Mr. Westwood never supported its mission—only now, as he sees its market value, does he claim interest. This isn't about equity. It's punishment masked as practicality," Julia counters.

"Is your client requesting alimony or any share of Mr. Westwood's assets?" The judge asks Julia, while taking some notes on a pad of paper.

"No, Your Honor. Mrs. Westwood is asking for nothing but the return of what she had before the marriage. She has declined spousal support and any claim on his holdings. She's asking to walk away with her name, her work, and her dignity intact," Julia answers.

"Mr. Westwood has had over a month to respond. No signed documents, no formal objections, no communication through legal channels. Why?" He leans forward knowing the answer could change everything for me.

"Your Honor, this case is personal. Mr. Westwood didn't respond immediately because he didn't want the marriage to end. He needed time—not just to review the filing, but to process what it meant. The silence wasn't obstruction. It was hope," Kendra says.

Hope? Really? I almost scoff at that. You have to truly love someone to have hope. Rhys never loved me. Only himself.

"Respectfully, Your Honor, there's a difference between grieving and leveraging silence. Mrs. Westwood filed clearly, formally, and calmly. There were no mixed signals. No ambiguity. Mr. Westwood's "hope" involved no legal response, no counsel outreach, and an effort to position himself to sell the petitioner's nonprofit asset behind her back," Julia counters.

"Mr. Westwood also has reason to believe the petitioner's motives were not solely about closure. Mrs. Westwood has an ongoing relationship with Mr. Owen Duvain—her sister's brother-in-law and a known former associate of her late father. Their personal connection predates the divorce filing, and evidence suggests the relationship may be sexual in nature," Kendra lets the ball drop.

What the fuck? That shitbag knows I'm not like that. But he sure as hell is! Do I have to remind everyone of his seven affairs?

"Your Honor, the implication here is not only speculative—it is beneath the dignity of this court. Mr. Duvain is not a party to this action. He is not married. There is no cohabitation, no financial entanglement, and no overlap with the marital timeline. Unlike Mr. Westwood, Mrs. Westwood did not drain joint accounts to support secret affairs," Julia fires back.

"The nature of the petitioner's relationship with Mr. Duvain—" Kendra tries again, but Julia cuts her off.

"—does not belong in this courtroom. My client found emotional safety with someone who didn't spend her marriage betraying her. The fact that she moved forward—quietly, privately, and with integrity—is not a flaw. It's a recovery. What the defense calls infidelity is survival. And the idea that a woman leaving an abusive, dishonest marriage must remain untouched to be credible? That is the real disgrace here," Julia finishes.

"Noted. Let's move forward," Judge Riviera says. "Mrs. Westwood has made clear her requests of no alimony, no marital claim. Only retention of the property held in trust prior to the marriage. Counsel, are there any additional disputes from the respondent?"

"Only the matter of Hearthlight's valuation and its potential as a shared asset. Mr. Westwood maintains that the property gained influence and credibility due to his social proximity during the marriage."

"Which is neither quantifiable nor legally binding. Mr. Westwood's "proximity" did not contribute to grant funding, operational development, or public reputation. He's not listed on a single record, board, or filing. His role was absent—until he saw dollar signs," Julia argues.

"So the court is left with one party refusing to sign, offering no legal objection, and making an unsubstantiated claim against nonprofit real estate that predates the marriage," he says.

"Correct, Your Honor," Julia says.

"We request the court grant additional time to prepare a formal objection, if necessary," Kendra adds.

"You'll have seven days. That is a courtesy, not a right. If no formal response is submitted by then, I will proceed with default judgment. The court does not entertain weaponized delays," Riviera says. "Next hearing in two weeks. Adjourned."

We all rise as the judge leaves. I look over to see Kendra and Rhys arguing in hushed tones.

"It's okay," Julia says, pulling my attention to her. "That actually went our way, believe it or not."

"Bella—" Rhys starts, walking towards me. Julia immediately steps in front of me so he can't get any closer.

"Mr. Westwood. Not here," Kendra says, stepping in and grabbing his arm. "Ms. Carter. If your client is willing, we'd like to schedule a private meeting. Discuss terms. A settlement."

Julia turns to me and I nod. This is hopefully a way we can just finish this. Be done with everything.

We walk to a room on the other side of the courthouse and go inside. It's just the four of us here. The room feels like it's closing in on me and I don't know how much more I can take.

Owen: *Breathe, Arabella.*

His voice slides through my mind. Grounding me somehow.

Owen: *It's just panic. Let it come. Let it pass.*

I dig my nails into my palms and clench my jaw.

Owen: *You're safe. I've got you.*

The mark on my skin warms faintly—barely a flicker. Like he's trying not to push, just letting me know that our bond is there and protecting me.

Owen: *Look at something solid. Focus on the floor. Feel your feet. Breathe in. Four counts. Out. Four counts.*

"To resolve this cleanly, Mr. Westwood is prepared to forfeit any claim to Hearthlight, effective immediately," Kendra says as we all sit down.

My hands aren't shaking anymore. The air doesn't feel like it's strangling me. I'm still tense, but the panic's dulled. It's manageable now. I don't hear Owen anymore. He knows that I'm okay, but I do send him a thank you through our bond anyway.

I can feel when he moves to the back of my mind. He's still there. He never leaves me completely.

"In exchange for?" Julia raises a brow.

"A nondisclosure agreement. Mrs. Westwood will not make public statements or written claims connecting the Creed family to any interference with her nonprofit or the divorce proceedings."

"You want her silence?" Julia retorts.

"They already had it. I wasn't talking about them then, and I'm not starting now," I say.

"Provided the NDA includes a mutual clause—no commentary from the Westwoods or Creeds either," Julia adds.

"Of course."

"Send the documents today. We'll sign within twenty four hours," Julia says.

"Once we receive those, Mr. Westwood will sign the divorce papers," Kendra adds.

Our chairs scrape as we push back. We leave the room and I feel free... I think.

"Bella—" Rhys comes running up behind me. Julia is right there, but she reads my face knowing that I have something to say.

"If you were worried about what I might say, maybe you should've worried about what you did," I say. I turn and walk away. I'm done. Julia will handle the rest. I never have to worry about Rhys Westwood again... hopefully.

I go straight to Hearthlight after the hearing. Julia recommended taking the day off, but I just didn't want to. This is one of my safe places. The other is with Owen.

"Hey, Bella!" Emery says, smiling from her new desk. "Everything work out?"

"The best it could," I respond. When I decided to hire an assistant, Emery was the first and last person I interviewed. She fit everything I needed and more. Plus she knows what I need, sometimes even before I need it.

"Tinsley wants to chat about something. She's in your office whenever you're ready for her."

"Okay! Thank you!" I exclaim.

Tinsley's just sitting in my office. Cream pantsuit. Tailored within an inch of its life. She's more put together than I am even on my best day.

"Hey, Tinsley. What's up?" I ask while taking off my coat and hanging it on the back of my chair.

"I was going over some of the numbers to get ready for what charity event we could do this year. They're not bad, but they could be better," she says.

"Define 'not bad'," I say cautiously. With everything that happened today, I don't want to deal with this now.

She shoots me an apologetic look, almost a wince.

I groan and rub my hands over my face. "You mean it's time for a fundraiser." she nods in response. "God, I hate galas. I hate asking."

"You're not asking for yourself." Tinsley's voice is kind and caring, it always is. "You're asking for them. And if it helps... I'll handle the ugly parts," she says.

"Sounds good to me," I grumble.

"What are you thinking about?" She asks, opening her laptop.

I have no idea. I don't do parties. I don't really love dressing up either. It's honestly something that makes me shiver. I'm glad Tinsley knows what she's doing because I'm always at a loss.

"I have some options. Maybe an Enchanted Garden? Masquerade? Casino Night? Maybe even Old Hollywood on the red carpet?"

"I don't know, Tinsley. They all sound... right. And wrong. I can't even think straight anymore," I say.

"We'll do the masquerade. The elegant version. Candlelight, velvet, gold trim—not theatrical. Symbolic," she says, clapping.

"Alright," I say. "I guess we're throwing a masquerade fundraiser."

Chapter Twelve
Owen

Bella decided that she wanted to cook tonight, she even brought over some of what she considered her absolute necessities—appliances and cookbooks. The excitement on her face made it completely impossible for me to tell her that I could simply conjure anything she wanted.

There's no stopping the grin that takes over my face when I walk through the door and hear her humming along to some song I've never heard. She's here, she's home with me. If I have it my way, she's never leaving.

I put my arms around her and pull her close, resting my chin on her shoulder watching her stir whatever she's making on the stove.

"What's for dinner?" I ask, kissing her neck.

"Now see you're distracting me." She giggles. "Spicy shrimp tacos with mango slaw. One of my favorites."

I look at the counter to see masa dusted all over the place. There are ingredients and tools everywhere.

"Is everything made from scratch?" I ask, lifting a brow.

"Yeah. I needed to get out of my head. Between the fundraising gala and Rhys, I'm overloaded," she says, still looking at the pot of beans.

"Speaking of the gala," I say, clearing my throat like I'm Mr. Darcy trying to work up the courage to talk to Elizabeth Bennet.. "Arabella, may I have the honor of escorting you to the fundraiser?"

She laughs, full and bright. "You may." Then she's in my arms, kissing me like I'm already her favorite dance.

Raymond: *Hey, Owen. Are you guys home? Julia needs to talk to Arabella.*

"I know that look," Bella says. "You getting a call?"

"Yeah, but from Raymond," I say. My brows knit together, and I know a dark look has taken over my face. This can't be good. "Julia needs to talk to you."

"Okay." She takes a deep, steadying breath and wipes her hands off on her apron.

Owen: *We're home. Are you going to portal over?*

Raymond: *We'll be there in a second.*

He means what he says because before I can tell Bella, they're coming, they're already in our living room.

"Hey guys," Julia says, practically bouncing as she steps into the room. "Sorry to bother you so late, but I wanted to give this to Bella."

She hands her a stack of papers. Emotions fly across her face too fast for anyone else to clock a single one—confusion, hope and then a joy so raw it nearly knocks the air out of me.

"What is it?" I ask.

"Rhys signed them." She cries out. "He signed the divorce papers!"

I grab her, lifting her right off the floor and twirling her in a rush of pure adrenaline. "Hell yes!"

She laughs into my neck, and I swear— for the first time since I've known her—she feels free.

"How much do I owe you?" Bella asks, turning to Raymond and Julia.

I slide my hand to hers, gentle but firm. "No," I say softly. "How much do *we* owe you?"

"Owen?" she breathes.

I don't hesitate. "The second that mark seared into your skin, you were mine. Not borrowed. Not temporary. *Mine.*"

Julia hands me the invoice and it looks wrong. There aren't any labor costs. Just basic court fees for what it costs to file the paperwork and the hearing.

"This can't be right," Bella says, looking at the invoice in my hands.

"No labor charge?" I ask.

"Not for a friend," she says, smiling. "We get each other in a way very few can understand, Bella. You were in a position I wouldn't wish on anyone. It was my pleasure to be able to help you."

Bella doesn't say a word—just crosses the room in three strides and throws her arms around Julia. The kind of hug that knocks the breath out of both of them. Her voice wavers when she finally speaks. "Thank you. God, thank you. I didn't think I'd ever feel this free."

"I'm ready to head back to my mate... and I think these two need some time. Maybe an infernal claim is happening sometime tonight?" Raymond says, winking at me.

"Infernal claim?" Bella asks.

"Oh I think we'll just let Owen explain it to you," Raymond says, laughing hard.

"We'll talk soon," Julia says, hugging Bella one last time.

They step back through Raymond's portal, leaving Bella and I alone together.

I take the plates out of the cabinet, noticing that they're red, Bella's favorite color. I place them, silverware, and wine glasses on the table just in time for Bella to bring in the food.

As Bella serves, she asks, "So Infernal claim huh?"

"Raymond is an idiot," I say, rolling my eyes.

"He is? Well what is it?" She asks, not meeting my eyes. *Is she...embarrassed?*

"Only the single most important thing in the soulmate bond," I say, letting out a sigh. "It's when you, as my soulmate, fully accept the bond."

"What does this entail?" She asks.

"It starts with the words," I murmur, voice thick.

She swallows hard, my eyes stare at her throat and I lick my lips.

"Next the Mark wakes up." I reach out, tracing the edge of her wrist with two fingers. "It won't ask. It won't wait. It'll burn through you—rip you open from the inside. Not to hurt you." I pause, letting the tension hang. "To *remake* you."

Her breath shivers past her lips. The candlelight flickers between us.

"You'll give it something precious," I continue. "A memory. A truth. Something innocent. And it'll take it, devour it, like it's been starving just for *you*."

She leans in. Just slightly. But I feel it.

"And when your body starts to break," I say, voice deepening, "when you're right at the edge of burning out—*that's* when I touch you."

She exhales my name. Barely audible.

I step between her knees, hands braced on the edge of her chair. "And when you do... you won't just bear the Mark. You'll be something new. *Mine*."

Her lips part. "Say it again."

"Mine," I growl, mouth close enough to kiss but not touching. "And if you let me, tonight—I'll show you exactly what that means."

"We can finish eating later," she says. Then pushes up and jumps into my arms, wrapping her legs around my waist.

Her mouth crashes into mine like she needs to taste everything she's been holding back.

I grip the back of her thighs, hoisting her deeper into me. She moans when I kiss her harder, and it hits me low, deep, like a fucking drug.

I walk us toward the bedroom—slow on purpose. I want her to feel every step. Every second of what she just chose.

Her fingers dig into my hair, pulling me down to her neck. "Owen..." she gasps, and I bite—just enough to make her gasp again.

"You don't know what you just started," I murmur against her skin, dragging my mouth along her jaw, tasting her pulse with my tongue.

She pulls back just enough to look at me, breathless, wrecked. "Show me."

Fuck.

I push the bedroom door open with my foot and press her against it, grinding into her as I kiss her like I've wanted to for months.

"Mine," I growl, nipping at her lower lip, then kissing the sound out of her mouth. "Say it."

"Yours," she gasps, rolling her hips against me. "God, *Owen.*"

I carry her to the bed, dropping her onto the mattress like I'm offering her up to every dark thing that lives in me before following her down.

I catch her wrists in one hand and press them above her head. My body pins hers to the mattress, my weight intentional, claiming. "Don't move," I say, my voice low and rough. "You give Greed an inch—he'll take your soul."

Her breath hitches. "Take it. All of it"

That's all it takes.

I kiss her like I'm starving. Lips bruising, tongue demanding, mouth moving with years of restraint turned to ash. Her legs wrap around me like instinct, her body arching into mine with a needy, breathless sound.

I sit back on my knees, eyes locked on hers as I hook my fingers under the hem of her shirt.

"Lift your arms," I murmur.

She obeys, breath trembling and I pull the fabric over her head, dragging it up like I'm peeling back something sacred. Her bare skin glows in the low light, flushed, waiting.

My hands skim her ribs, trailing down to the waistband of her leggings. "These too," I say, voice thick. "I want nothing between us."

She raises her hips and I take my time—sliding them down inch by inch, kissing the newly exposed skin as I go. Her thighs, her knees, her calves. Reverent. Addicted.

When she's bare beneath me, I just look. Let the moment stretch. Let her feel how badly I want her.

"Perfect," I whisper, dragging my gaze back up her body. "Every inch of you."

I drag my mouth down her neck, biting, sucking, marking her in ways she'll still feel tomorrow. My hands follow—palming her breasts, teasing her nipples until she's whimpering beneath me.

I push her thighs apart with my knee, slipping my hand between them. She's already soaked, heat pulsing, back bowing off the bed.

"You're dripping for me," I growl into her skin. "And I haven't even fucked you yet."

I rub tight circles over her clit, just enough pressure to make her gasp. Her hips roll in time with my hand, breath coming faster, eyes glazed over.

"Owen—please—"

"Shh," I whisper against her mouth. "You begged me to take you. Let me."

She's soaked and ready, thighs open like a prayer, and I don't hesitate. I drive into her in one hard, claiming thrust.

Her body arches. She gasps, fingers digging into my shoulders.

I catch her wrists and pin them above her head, pressing her down into the mattress. "No. You don't touch me. You *take* me."

"Owen—"

"You wanted Greed. Don't whimper now."

I move—rough, deep strokes that make the bed frame groan and her breath hitch with every thrust.

"So fucking tight," I mutter, grinding into her. "Like your body's trying to keep me. Own me."

My pace turns brutal. Controlled only by the restraint that's about to snap. She's moaning now, shaking, her thighs trembling around me.

"This is what you asked for," I say, voice raw. "No softness. No mercy. Just me, *inside you*, until you don't remember who you were before I touched you."

Her mouth falls open. "Owen—please—fuck—"

I slam into her harder. "Don't beg. You already gave yourself to me."

She cries out, coming hard, clenching around me so tight it rips the air from my lungs. I don't stop. I chase it—like I'm starving, like it's never going to be enough.

"I want more," I snarl. "Your scream. Your surrender. Your fucking soul."

"It's yours," she chokes out. "It's always been yours."

I come with a guttural groan, burying myself so deep it feels like I'm trying to brand her from the inside. Maybe I am. My release hits hard, sharp, endless.

When it's over, I stay inside her, breath heavy, one hand wrapped around her throat.

"You're mine now," I whisper. "I don't give things back."

Chapter Thirteen

Arabella

I wake up cocooned in Owen's arms. Like, fully wrapped. One arm under me, one across me, leg thrown over mine like he's trying to keep me from escaping in my sleep.

He's a cuddler. A serious one.

Which is hilarious, honestly. You wouldn't look at Owen—the walking embodiment of smolder and sin—and think, oh yeah, that guy definitely needs to be the little spoon sometimes.

But here we are.

As much as I would love to stay here, I can't. I have to get to Hearthlight. It's Wednesday—intake day.

We have four apartments open this week. It's more than we've had in a while, which is great news. But it also means it's going to be a busy day... for everyone.

I try to roll out of Owen's arms, but he has me caged. I'm not going anywhere without waking him up first.

"Owen," I say. "Wake up." Nothing. Just a soft snore in response. "Owen!" I say louder this time.

"What? What?" He startles, blinking and tightening his grip on me.

I laugh. "I have to get up. Think you can release me?"

He does, and when I get up, I feel sore. Not in a bad way.

Actually—in an incredible way.

Every feeling is still etched into my muscles. Branded on my bones. Like he rewrote my body with every touch and left a signature under my skin.

I can still hear him. *"Shh. You begged me to take you. Let me."*

The way his fingers gripped my wrist. His body claimed mine. I don't want to lose that feeling. In fact, I want to feel that way every single night.

My legs protest when I move. I feel... wrecked. In the best possible way. He ripped me to shreds and stitched me back together with his passion. He knew what I could take. And when I would break.

"What are you thinking about?"

I look over to Owen. He's sitting up in bed, staring at me standing in front of him with nothing more than a sheet wrapped around my body.

"You have this glazed look in your eyes." His lips tilt at the corners into a lazy smirk.

"Just thinking," I say, trying to play it cool.

"I think I know," he jokes. "You had the same look in your eyes last night when you... you know."

"Shut up!" I laugh, throwing a pillow at him. "I need to get ready."

I don't wait for a response and head straight to the bathroom. There are red towels, and all my favorite products.

"Hey," I say, showing Owen a bottle of shampoo. "When did you find time to get all my favorites?"

"Ophelia helped a lot, but I want you to feel at home here," he says.

I grin and dart into the bathroom. No time to linger—I'm already late. I shower and throw on some clothes.

When I head back into the bedroom, Owen is out of bed. I'll be honest, my heart drops, I thought he would have stayed for a bit, said goodbye, something after the night we had. My worries melt away when I find him in the kitchen.

"Breakfast for the road?" he says, handing me a muffin.

"Okay, weird question," I start.

"Shoot," he says, turning slightly toward me.

"If you can conjure anything you want, why do you have clothes? A kitchen? Like—why even cook?"

He shrugs. "Sometimes normalcy is nice. I grew up with a kitchen. So did my cousins. Our moms were mortal once too."

He hands me a napkin, like he's done this a thousand times. "They raised us to know we might have mortal mates—and that we should build something that makes sense to them too."

"What time is it?" I ask.

"7:55," he says, looking at the mortal clock.

"I'm going to be late!" I run up, giving Owen a quick kiss. "I'll see you later."

I'm getting good at conjuring portals and when I do, I end up right in my apartment thankfully. Without hesitation or even looking around, I open the front door and run down to my office. Emery is at her desk already.

As I approach, she looks up. "Hey, Bella." I stop in my tracks and look at her. "What's wrong?"

"How could you possibly...?" Her eyes go wide as she meets my gaze

"I know you, Emery. So what's wrong?"

"My boyfriend and I broke up. I thought he was going to propose." She lets out a hollow laugh. "Turns out, he was just planning his exit."

"Oh Emery! I'm so sorry," I say. "If you need a day—" She cuts me off.

"No. I'm okay. Better off without the loser anyway. Plus we have a ton of work to do today."

The morning flies by. I'm buried in intake folders and CPS emails. Everyone wants updates. That's why Wednesdays are our craziest days.

After a couple of hours, I need a break for a few minutes. I need to think, wrap my mind around everything that's happening, not just here, but in my personal life as well. Just five minutes with my door shut. I need to think.

I sit in my chair and put my head back, closing my eyes. I can feel a migraine coming on. My focus lasers back to the present when I hear Emery's voice accompanied by some shouts from the front.

"I said you can't just walk in—"

I don't hear the rest because my door is pushed open so hard it knocks against the wall.

In comes the Creeds. Or Ellison, Tierney, and Sterling to be exact.

Tierney Creed is striking—elegant in a bone-colored coat and cream silk blouse, every inch polished perfection. But it's her face that stops me.

Because for a second, I swear I'm looking at Tinsley.

The same sharp cheekbones, the same almond-shaped eyes. Her hair's darker, styled in waves, but the resemblance is unmistakable.

Tinsley has her mother's face.

"May I help you?" I ask, keeping my tone calm and professional. I'm not going to let these people rattle me.

That's when I see someone walk in behind them. Rhys. God why can't this man go away?

"Bella," he says.

"Arabella," I correct. He doesn't get to have a personal connection to me. Not anymore.

"Oh come on! Seriously?" He exclaims.

"May I help you?" I ask again. Ignoring Rhys completely.

"We're here to bring Tinsley home. This... nonprofit stint has run its course. She was never meant to work herself to death in a place like this," Ellison says in a condescending tone.

"You've got her wasting Ivy League credentials chasing down food pantry donations. She belongs at Creed Holdings, not in a glorified halfway house," Sterling adds.

"We're not here to make trouble. Just offering a way out," Rhys says. His tone is unreadable. I don't know what he's trying to do. If he is trying to help the Creeds or... hurt me. Either one is not in my favor.

"But if she insists on staying... maybe there's a way we can work together. You've done well here, Arabella. It'd be a shame for this place to stay stuck in... modesty. We could invest. Turn it into something profitable" Ellison says.

"Real estate like this? We're offering a lifeline. You could expand. Upgrade. Stop scraping for grants and pocket change," Sterling says.

I say nothing. Active listening is an important skill in my line of work. But it comes in handy when dealing with narcissists like Ellison and Sterling Creed. They will talk themselves into digging their own grave.

"Look, if it's about pride, we get it. But Tinsley doesn't belong here. She's family. We're taking her home," Sterling says, switching the subject back to his sister since talking about the building isn't working.

"This isn't her life, Arabella. She doesn't understand what she's giving up. She was never meant for—this," Ellison says, turning more forceful against me.

"Funny you say that. Since you're the ones who sold her soul to begin with." I let that little tidbit hang in the air.

By the slight distressed look on their faces, I can tell they weren't expecting me to have any knowledge of that. To their credit, they hid it well. A gasp by the door captures my attention. Tierney's face says it all. Confusion. She had no idea her husband had sold her daughter's soul.

"You don't know what you're talking about," Sterling says. He's defensive, but the cockiness hasn't gone away.

"It was a temporary exchange for long term gain," Ellison says. He waves his hand away like it's no big deal.

"You sold her soul. There's nothing *temporary* about that," I counter. "Interesting that you don't ask how I know this. I guess Rhys told you everything."

"Wait—what does she mean? Ellison?" Her voice cracks. She steps back, like distance will protect her.

"What does Bella mean?" Her voice is filled with more anger than I've heard from her, more anger than I thought possible.

I will the door to the front of my office to close and lock.

Arabella: *Owen, can you portal to my office?*

I don't wait for a response. I can feel that he heard me.

"See what my lovely ex husband didn't know or tell you..." I trail off. "Is that my fated mate is the demon who made the deal."

Not even a second later, Owen's charcoal black portal appears and he enters through it.

Rhys leans against the wall, but I can see him flinch. He wouldn't want another run in with a Duvain. Sterling and Ellison are taken back in stunned silence. Tierney screams on the top of her lungs.

"Who... what is that?" Tinsley sputters out.

Emery is dead quiet, but her mouth is hanging open. She doesn't wait another second before turning around and running out of the room.

"Did you need something, Belladonna?" Owen asks.

Rhys recoils. "Jesus. That's what you call her?" He makes a face, eyes narrowing. "You know that's literally poison, right? Belladonna?

Deadly nightshade? A gorgeous plant that creeps into your system until you can't breathe."

He scoffs, shaking his head. "Makes sense. If you want a woman like Arabella, you must have a thing for women that ruin you."

"What's pathetic is you still being obsessed with her while the Creeds lead you around by your dick," Owen retorts, smile razor sharp. He turns his attention to Ellison. "You made a deal. You thought I'd forget?"

The shadows around him thicken. The overhead light flickers. The air presses down, heavy, charged like a storm caught in a sealed room.

"You trafficked your own blood. Bartered your daughter's soul like a line item."

Tierney stumbles back against the desk. Sterling's jaw clenches, lips bloodless.

"You think I care about your money? Your titles? I am what waits when your last deal runs dry." Owen steps forward and the floor creaks under his power. "Try to take her," he growls, voice laced with something that doesn't sound human. "And I'll make you beg for Hell. Because at least there, someone might remember your name. See here's the thing. You probably don't know this, but Ophelia and Bella had another sister. Cassius traded Ophelia for her success. But at the end of it all, she was wiped from existence. No one remembers her. Poof... she was gone. I will celebrate the day this happens to you."

Ellison grabs for Tinsley's wrist—but his hand doesn't reach. He's frozen mid motion, trembling, locked in place like the very room turned against him.

Owen whispers, "Go ahead. Touch her. See what I do."

Ellison yanks back his arm like it's burned.

"We're done," Sterling snaps. "You want to stay in this sewer? With *them*? Fine."

Ellison's glare cuts through the room. "But understand this, Tinsley—if you don't walk out with us right now, you're no longer a Creed."

Tinsley doesn't even flinch. "Then disown me." Her voice is ice. "Because you already signed me away the day you signed that contract."

He doesn't shout. He doesn't tremble. He says it like a verdict. "You're disowned. Don't come back."

They leave Tinsley with me. Emery closes the door behind them.

"Good riddance I say!" Emery exclaims. "Now Bella... fated mate? You have some serious explaining to do!"

"Uhhh you don't seem shocked by all of this," Tinsley says.

"Because it's so cool!" Emery shouts, throwing her hands in the air.

"You're not concerned that Owen or any other demons could hurt you? Us?" Tinsley asks, her suspicion clear in her tone.

"Please if they were going to, they would have. Plenty of chances and all!"

"I need some explanations," Tinsley says, turning to us.

Owen takes a breath, his tone matter-of-fact. "Ellison wanted office. Not just mayor—governor, eventually senator. He wanted his name carved into buildings, stamped on laws, whispered in backrooms like royalty."

He paces slowly, voice like a lit fuse. "Sterling? He wanted developments. Power. Real estate. To turn every plot of this city into profit. He didn't want influence—he wanted control."

"So they summoned me. Not just any demon—a Duvain. They used rites given to them by Arabella and Ophelia's father, twisted into something barely functional, but just enough to get my attention." Owen stops, the air around him humming with power. "When I asked for their price? They gave me you."

Tinsley shakes her head, but it's slower this time. "No... They wouldn't. They couldn't." Her voice falters. "They love me. They're strict, yeah, but... they've always looked out for me. Paid for school. Made sure I was—" She stops. The words die in her throat. Her eyes flick toward the door they left through.

"They wouldn't just... throw me away."

Owen doesn't answer. He doesn't need to.

Tinsley presses her hand to her chest like it physically hurts. "They already did," I say.

That's when she breaks. Her knees buckle before anyone can stop her. The sound that rips from her chest isn't just a sob—it's a howl. Emery's the first to catch her, arms wrapping tight as Tinsley crumples into a shaking, gasping heap on the floor. "No, no, no," she chokes out. "I didn't even do anything—why wasn't I enough?"

Her voice is raw, shattered glass scraping down her throat.

I drop to the floor beside them, pulling both of them into my arms like I'm trying to piece the broken girl back together.

"You are," I whisper fiercely, forehead pressed to Tinsley's. "You are more than enough."

Tinsley shakes her head, fists balled in Emery's shirt. "They were supposed to protect me. They were supposed to love me. They said I was their favorite. They said I was the best of us." The heartbreak in her voice is unbearable.

Emery presses her cheek to Tinsley's temple, tears slipping down her face. "You are the best of us. That's why they feared losing you."

"They don't get to define love anymore," I say, my voice cracking but unshaken. "We do. Right here. This room. We've got you."

Tinsley sobs harder, body shaking like the grief is tearing muscle from bone.

Emery brushes her hair back gently, smoothing it with trembling fingers. "You're not alone, Tins. You never will be again."

"But I'm not free, am I?" Tinsley's voice is soft, brittle.

Owen doesn't look away. "No. That deal is real."

"It's binding?" Her eyes lift to his, hollow with disbelief.

"It is," he says, voice like stone. "Your soul was offered and marked."

Bella shifts closer, her tone sharp. "What if we do what Ophelia did? The same ritual, the same blood oath—"

"You can't," Owen says, voice certain. "Ophelia gave her soul. That gave her power—she chose it, willingly, to save Julian. That kind of sacrifice rewrites the contract. But yours," he looks at Tinsley, "was stolen. You never chose it. And that makes it harder to undo."

Tinsley lets out a breath that's more laugh than sound. It's bitter. Small. "So I'm doomed."

"No," Owen says, without hesitation.

She looks up, eyes rimmed red. "Feels like it."

"We'll take it to the council," Owen says.

"The council?" She asks.

"If anyone can undo what they did to you—it's them." Owen's eyes glint like polished obsidian as he turns to me. "Pack your fire, sweetheart. We're going to Hell."

Chapter Fourteen
Owen

I could ask the Infernal Council, but I asked Ophelia to talk to them about a meeting. She is closer with them than anyone and probably can convince them of the urgency of this.

Once I got the all clear, I brought everyone to Hell.

Tinsley was nervous, that's to be expected. Not many mortals walk into Hell unless they're bound to one of us... or already dead.

But Hell doesn't scorch first. It stuns. The obsidian peaks, the rivers of silver fire, the sky stitched with blood red stars. It opens like a cathedral built on sin.

And Tinsley? She didn't scream. She stared. Awestruck.

I watched her take it all in, jaw slack, eyes wide, and felt the smallest pulse of satisfaction.

It's slightly funny, if you think about it. It doesn't take us long to reach the cathedral.

Before we go any further, I turn to Tinsley and hold out a hand to stop her. "We need to go over some ground rules."

"Owen..." Bella warns.

"No, Bella," I cut in, firm. "She needs to know. And so do you."

I cross my arms. "The Infernal Council isn't a mortal court. You don't talk back. You don't argue. You show respect. Their word is final."

Bella starts to move forward. I block her path. "No, Owen," she snaps. "They'll listen to us."

"I won't let you in there if you don't understand what's at stake!" I shout.

"Let me in there? Seriously?" She shoves at me, anger flaring. "I know what's at stake—Tinsley's soul!"

She tries to push past me, but the doors don't budge.

Because they didn't summon her. I requested this meeting with them, no one summons the council. She can't get in unless I open them.

"I'll open the doors," I say, lowering my voice. "But please... Bella. This isn't a mortal trial. This is Hell. Your rules—your honor—they don't work here. If Tinsley's soul is going to be saved, *she* has to fight for it."

"Which means," I add gently, "you can't speak."

She stares at me. Burning. Brimming with words she can't use.

"Fine..." she mutters. But I know her. She's gnawing at the bit. And she won't stay quiet forever.

I put my hand on the door and feel the tendrils of magic circling my arm, making it glow with runes.

The doors open with a creak. Inside the chamber is inconceivably vast with no walls in sight. It's empty. There is a place for us. It's carved into the obsidian on the floor. A massive circle etched deep into the obsidian, glowing faintly with molten red lines. Intricate runes spiral outward from the center—some demonic, some ancient mortal languages long forgotten.

I walk Bella and Tinsley to a specific section.

"Are we early?" Tinsley asks.

"We're right on time," I say. "They'll come. We enter first. They always enter last."

We wait for a few minutes before I feel it. Blue fire circles around us. Coming closer until it's almost engulfing us.

Seven figures materialize all at once. Tinsley gasps as she sees the hooded, faceless figures.

"What is the meaning of this urgent meeting, Owen Duvain?" They all say.

"I've brought forth a mortal under binding contract. Her soul was traded without consent. We seek counsel. Options for her," I say, bowing my head,

I hear grumbling and I know that they're speaking to one another. I knew this could be a long shot, but if there's a chance, we need to take it.

"That is not your jurisdiction," they say. "She is not your mate."

"No. She is under the protection of the House of Duvain," I say.

Bella has no idea what I just did. The council does, though. The flames raise in the air crashing down like water flowing around us. Being under a family or house's protection is major. No one really does it anymore, and even then it was incredibly rare. Julian alluded to it when it came to Bella, but I said it outright. To the council no less.

"The mortal may speak," they say, their haunting voices echoing through the space.

Tinsley steps forward to where a hooded arm gestured her to go. Her hands may be shaking, but her spine is ramrod straight. She would never let them see her sweat.

"My name is Tinsley Creed. My father and brother sold my soul in a deal I never knew about. I didn't agree. I didn't consent. I want to fight for my soul back," she says.

"You cannot choose your bloodline. But you live with what it surrenders," they say.

"Please," she begs. "There has to be something. I'll do anything!"

"There is nothing for you to do. Your family sold your soul. Only great sacrifice can rectify it," they say.

"What do I need to sacrifice?" I can see the hope blooming in Tinsley's eyes. I know this is not going to end well. Sacrifice is what Julian did for Bella or Ophelia for Julian. There is no way a Creed would do that for love. They only love themselves.

"You helped Ophelia. Why won't you help Tinsley?" Bella asks, stepping up with a dangerous indignation in her eyes.

"Ophelia offered something irreplaceable. Her sacrifice was made in love and blood. This one offers desperation alone," they say.

"That's bullshit! You want cost? Her whole life has been taken. Her choice, her soul—gone! Thrown away like garbage!" Bella screams.

"You are not permitted to speak," they say, their voices rising. I've never seen them angry before, and I desperately do not want to. Not at my mate.

"No," Bella's voice rises. She throws her hands in the air. "I'm the only one here saying what no one else will. You call this justice? You're cowards are hiding behind rituals while men sell their daughters like property and you look away!"

"Bella... stop," I say, stepping up to grab her arm, to make her see the mistake she's making. "It's about balance."

"No, Owen! It's about what's right!" Bella exclaims. "You think you're powerful? You're outdated and useless."

"You overstep. You insult this council with mortal arrogance and greed. Mercy is not a right. Favor is not a birthright," they say.

"Bella! Enough!" I step in front of her, cutting her off from the council. I can feel her anger through our mark.

"Control your soulmate, Owen Duvain," they say.

"She doesn't understand." I bow my head to them.

"I understand that unless they're branded or sold, they don't matter to these fuckers," she mutters under her breath.

I'm pretty sure that was the worst possible thing she could have said. She probably just destroyed everything I've built with the council. I wasn't expecting them to do this.

"House Duvain's favor is revoked. As is Ophelia's. You may not petition this court again. Not by name. Not by blood," they say.

"But—" I sputter.

"Owen Duvain... your seal is rescinded. You no longer hold the right to contract or claim in our name. Your authority in the Infernal Accord is dissolved," they say.

I go rigid—every part of me pulled taut, locked up, refusing to believe what I just heard. But the power inside me? It's gone. Hollowed out like someone scooped out my spine and left me standing in the shell.

My knees hit the floor with a crack that echoes in my bones. I can't breathe. My seal—my name—what I am... gone.

This isn't a punishment. It's an execution.

"Your legacy is broken. Your power, revoked. You will not trade. You will not bind. Not again." They disappear in blue flames leaving.

The fire that used to burn in my veins is cold now. I don't know who I am without it.

They stripped me down to ash.

And Bella—she made it happen.

"What the fuck were you thinking!" I scream at Bella. "I told you to be respectful!"

"Owen—I—" She says, eyes wide.

"No, Arabella! Just no! You took everything from me, my family, your sister. For what? Righteousness in a right that was never yours or mine?"

"That's not fair! It *is* our fight! You made the deal!" She screams.

My eyes flash, voice like a whip cracking against the wall. "You think that justifies it? That's because I made the deal, it's yours to undo?"

She steps forward. "Tinsley's my friend. I *had* to try—"

"No," I snap. "If you wanted to try, you would have listened to me! Do what I told you to do! You would have listened to the one person who knew what the fuck we were walking into!"

Bella's breath stutters.

"You always think you know better," I say. "Always *righteous*, always *louder*, always the one to kick down the door. But this wasn't yours to fight. Not like that."

"I couldn't stand by and do *nothing*," she says, voice breaking.

I lean in, low and bitter. "You didn't stand by. You stood *in the way*."

She recoils like I slapped her.

I shake my head, fury replaced with disappointment. "You weren't trying to save her, Arabella. You were trying to rewrite the world to fit what *you* thought was fair. That's not justice. That's true greed."

She turns away from me. I can feel her heart breaking, but it doesn't matter. I thought we had the perfect life. It was harder than I thought. This isn't the life I want to live.

"I'm sorry," Tinsley says. "I caused all of this."

"You didn't," I say. I can barely look at Bella at this point.

"I can't stay in my apartment," Tinsley says. "Not after today. My father pays for it. I just... I can't."

"You don't have to," Bella says, her voice numb. "You can stay at my place."

"Emery has said in the past I can stay with her. She has a two bed two bath. I think I'll take her up on that," Tinsley says.

"Okay," I say. "I'll drop Arabella back at her place and we'll clean your apartment."

"My apartment? Not your place?" She asks, whipping her head towards me.

"I need some space," I say, simply.

She doesn't say anything, just nods.

Owen: *Julian can you meet us at the cathedral?*

Julian: *Sure... I'm on my way.*

By the time we walk out, Julian is already there, just below the steps waiting

"Can you take Arabella back to her place while we go to Tinsley's to clean her stuff out?" I ask.

"Why do you want me to drop Bella off?" Julian says, looking between the two of us.

"Not now. Please just not now. Ready Tinsley?" I ask.

"Owen—" Bella tries again, but I just can't.

I open a portal of my own and drag Tinsley through it to her apartment. All I had to tell her was to think about it.

We land inside her apartment. No—her prison disguised as luxury. High ceilings. Polished marble floors. Designer furniture no one sits in. Art chosen by decorators, not by her. It's all perfect. And soulless.

She freezes in the middle of the room. Doesn't touch a thing.

"This isn't me," she says softly.

"No," I say. "It never was."

Owen: *Need everyone at Tinsley's place. Track where I am to find it.*

They portal within minutes. I see Julian, Seth, Damian, Adrian, and Ophelia.

"Lucas and Caleb?" I ask.

"Out. Said they'd come if they can," Julian replies.

"This is Tinsley Creed. You know what happened. Her father owns this apartment. She needs out. Everything she wants goes. Leave what her father owns," I say.

"Come on, Tinsley," Ophelia says. "I can pack with you."

She looks around me and furrows her brow. I know she wants to ask about Bella, but Julian's slight shake of his head stops her. She nods and walks to the bedroom with Tinsley.

None of them say anything at first. They don't have to. We all felt it—the moment the Council severed our ties. The moment power shifted.

Finally, Julian speaks. "What happened?"

I exhale through my nose. "Bella."

"Define that." Damian tilts his head.

I pace the edge of the living room. My hands won't stop clenching.

"She walked into the chamber like a mortal courtroom," I say, voice tight. "Didn't wait. Didn't listen. She interrupted the Council. Challenged them. *Accused* them."

Julian doesn't speak. Just watches me from the arm of the couch, fingers steepled, face unreadable.

"They gave warnings," I go on. "Clear, direct warnings. She ignored them. Called them cowards. Said they let mortals rot in contracts they should've stopped. I tried to stop her."

Seth's arms are crossed, jaw flexing. "And they shut the door."

I laugh—sharp, bitter. "No. They *locked* it. They stripped me of my rights. My deals. Ophelia's loom was moved. Our access? Gone."

Damian exhales through his nose. "She tried to change the rules."

"She acted like the rules didn't apply to her," I say, dragging a hand through my hair. "Like her intentions would be enough."

Adrian speaks for the first time, quiet but grounded. "You love her."

I glare at him. "That doesn't excuse this."

"I'm not saying it does," he replies. "But maybe it's why it hurts this much."

I stop pacing. The rage still thrums under my skin, but now it's tangled in something else—grief.

Julian finally leans forward, resting his elbows on his knees. "She was wrong, Owen. But she wasn't malicious. She thought she was protecting Tinsley."

"She wasn't protecting *anyone*," I snap. "She was trying to win. She needed to be the hero."

Damian watches me carefully. "She made a mistake. A huge one. But punishing yourself for it doesn't undo it."

"I'm not punishing myself."

Seth lifts a brow. "Aren't you? You're furious because she cost you everything. But you're more furious because it was *her*."

I don't respond.

Julian's voice lowers. "You've got every right to be angry. But don't turn your back on her if there's still something worth saving."

I close my eyes. My fists are still clenched.

"She betrayed everything we are."

Adrian shrugs. "Maybe it's her turn to earn her way back in."

"No," I say, too fast.

Julian raises a brow.

"She's your soulmate."

"I know," I snap, the words punching out of me. "I *know*."

I drag in a breath, jaw tight. "But right now? I wish she wasn't."

No one pushes. No one tells me I don't mean it—because part of me does. The part that's still smarting from the Council's judgment, from watching everything I've built turned to ash because the woman I love couldn't just stay quiet.

Julian finally leans back again. "You've got two choices. Cut her out and walk forward with the damage... or let her try to fix what she broke."

"I'll forgive her," I say. "Eventually. But the Council? They won't. And I'm not sure I should, either. What she cost us, that isn't something you walk back with an apology."

"What do you want us to do?" Julian asks.

"We fight for it. We remind them why the Duvain name meant something. Why they put us in power in the first place." I lift my chin.

"You want to challenge the Council?" Damian's brow rises.

"I want to make them remember," I say. "Remember what it meant to have us on their side. To fear losing us."

Adrian crosses his arms. "We need to start planning. We rebuild from the inside out."

"They may have shut the door," I say, voice steel. "But they forgot—we built the fucking house."

Chapter Fifteen
Arabella

Julian takes me back to my old apartment. I don't call it home. Owen is home. His house is home.

I have no idea why he snapped at me. The audacity that he had to call me greedy. I was doing everything I can to help someone else... someone that is not myself. How in the world is that greedy?

"What happened, Bella?" Julian asks.

"I have no idea," I say. "I don't know what got into Owen."

"I'll talk to him." He assures me. I can tell by the furrowing of his brow that he's confused. "This isn't like him."

He drops me off at my front door and immediately leaves. I haven't been here in so long that I forgot about how small and dark this hallway is.

I pat my pockets to find my keys. *Fuck*. I don't have them. I gave them to Josie. Honestly, I never thought I was coming back. Letting out a sigh, I slump to the ground and bury my head in my hands, I guess happily ever afters don't exist. Not for me anyway.

"I feel like an idiot," I mutter. No, I cannot go down like this, standing up and squaring my shoulders, I knock on the door to my old life.

Josie opens the door, just as stunned to see me as I am to be here. Apparently, my resolve isn't as strong as I thought, at the sight of her I lose it—full on, ugly crying. Right there on my doorstep.

"What the hell?!" Josie exclaims. "Bells! What are you doing here?"

She pulls me into the apartment and on the couch, holding me close. "What happened?"

Great... that only makes me cry harder.

"Bad question. Got it," she says, holding me in her arms for what feels like hours before I can speak.

"Thank you." I choke out.

"Ready to tell me what happened?" She asks, rubbing my hair and speaking in a motherly tone. Honestly, I don't know what I'd do without this woman.

I exhale hard, dragging my hands through my hair. "I told the truth."

She arches a brow. "That's... vague."

"I told the truth," I repeat. "To a bunch of faceless, flaming assholes who pretend to care about justice but would rather watch girls get sold like cattle than lift a finger."

Josie doesn't interrupt.

I keep going. "Tinsley was amazing. Brave. She stood there shaking, and she still begged for her soul. And you know what they said? Nothing. Too late. Your dad sold you. Not our problem. So yeah—I spoke. Because someone had to."

"And Owen?"

I bite the inside of my cheek. "Lost his magic. His seal. His fancy Council privileges. All of it."

Josie winces.

I throw up my hands. "Don't look at me like that. I didn't mean for that to happen. But what was I supposed to do—just stand there while they humiliated her? Tell her to take it and smile?"

She stays quiet, so I fill the silence. "Owen said I was greedy. That I wanted to win. That I wasn't saving her—I was rewriting the world to fit what I thought was fair. And maybe I was. But I'd rather break the rules than watch another girl get broken."

I stand up and start pacing, letting out a scoff. "You know what's wild? He warned me not to talk. He stood right there, in front of the doors, and told me to shut up. And when I didn't? When I refused to be another silent witness? He acted like I betrayed *him*." I shake my head, fingers tightening into fists.

My laugh is brittle. "Like it was *me* who destroyed everything—not the council, not the system that lets fathers sell daughters, not the cosmic joke of 'justice' that only exists for people with power. No. It was me. Because I spoke."

I look at Josie and I don't like what I see. She is going to tell me something that I don't want to hear. I know it.

Josie folds her arms. "You always think you know what's best." I flinch, because yeah—she's not wrong. "You did what you believed was right. I know that. But this time... it wasn't just about Tinsley. You walked in there like you were the only one who could fix it. Like no one else's voice mattered unless it came through you."

I start to argue, but she barrels on. "You didn't trust Owen. You didn't even trust Tinsley until the Council gave her permission to speak. You went in with a plan, and when it didn't go your way, you bulldozed it. Now you're pissed that Owen couldn't stop the fallout."

"So what—he was right to call me greedy?" I whip my head towards her, putting my hands on my hips.

Josie shakes her head. "He didn't mean selfish. He meant you wanted control. You couldn't stand watching something awful happen without stepping in and rerouting the entire system. Even if it meant taking down everyone around you."

She stands in front of me. "You're not the villain, Bella. But you're not the victim here either."

That hits harder than anything Owen said. "I wasn't trying to control anything."

Josie lifts one brow, but doesn't say a word.

"I wasn't," I repeat. "I just... couldn't let them walk all over her."

"You didn't let them," Josie says gently. "You *rushed* them."

I shake my head, standing. "So what, I should've stood there like Owen? Bowed my head and played the game?"

"I'm saying maybe it wasn't your game to play."

I cross my arms, bite the inside of my cheek. "Well, maybe if Owen had backed me up instead of acting like I ruined his perfect Council résumé, we wouldn't even be having this conversation."

That's easier to say than admitting she might be right. Easier than thinking about the look on his face when the portal disappeared.

"You're not ready to hear it. That's okay. But you're going to have to—eventually," she says honestly. It's hard to tell if she pities me or is being straight with me. "I'm spending the night with my new boyfriend. I'll let you have the place to yourself. Maybe it'll give you some time to think."

She grabs an overnight bag that I didn't even see, and leaves in a rush. The disappointed look she gives me makes me wince. *Not pity. Disappointment. Even worse than I thought.*

When the door clicks and the dust settles, it sets in that I'm alone, truly alone with my thoughts. That's not where I want to be.

The room feels too still, like I've been dropped into a glass box and any single breath might shatter it.

I start pacing.

"I did what I had to do," I mutter to myself, to the room, to no one. My voice sounds warped. "They weren't going to help her. No one was going to help her."

She was alone.

"She would've walked out of there with nothing. Nothing. If I hadn't said something."

I saved her. Even though nothing came out of it anyway.

I laugh—a quick, dry sound that doesn't reach my eyes. "God, Owen acts like I marched in there with a sword. I *spoke.* I used my voice. That's not a crime."

But it feels like one. The rock sitting on my chest says otherwise. I press my hand to my sternum like I can physically hold it in.

"He should've stood with me. He *knew* the Council was corrupt. He *knew* I was right."

Okay so maybe the Council isn't corrupt, but they sure as shit seem like it to me!

I spin, catching my reflection in the mirror. My eyes are too wide. There's color in my cheeks—flushed from adrenaline or shame, I don't know. I look... unhinged.

"No. No, this is them. This is the system. I didn't destroy anything. They did. I just exposed it."

That's what justice is. It's messy. It's loud. It's uncomfortable.

I press my fingers to my temples. *So why did he look at me like I was a stranger?*

I sit down. Stand back up. Sit again. "Maybe I pushed too hard," I whisper.

But that's what you do when no one listens.

"Maybe I should've said less."

But they would have ignored you.

I stare at the floor. The same thought hits me again, but now it won't leave.

I didn't save her. Not really.

Tinsley didn't get to save her soul. Owen had everything that he has worked for his entire, impossibly long life taken away from him. I didn't fix anything. I just walked in there righteous and full of myself like I was the one person who knew it all. The fixer.

My voice breaks, soft now. "I didn't mean to ruin it."

But intentions don't matter, do they?

I can still feel Owen's power disappearing like a thread snapping inside me.

Because of me.

For the first time... I don't know how to fix it.

Arabella: *Owen?*

I feel the link close, it didn't flicker or weaken. It slammed shut.

He shut me out.

I try again, instinctively, like banging on a door someone just bolted in your face.

Nothing.

He's made a decision. I'm not worth hearing out. My throat tightens. I want to scream. I want to *apologize*.

Anger flares up like a second heartbeat. He should hear me out. I'm his soulmate. Doesn't that matter? I would never shut him out like this.

Would I?

Isn't that exactly what I did?

I shoved him aside, took control. I acted like my voice mattered more than his, in a place where I had no business being, no less. No wonder he doesn't want to talk to me. He asked for space. I bulldozed through that, too.

My heart is racing, my breath is coming in short bursts. My emotions are flying through me too fast for me to feel, let alone identify.

We're supposed to talk it out. *Fight* it out. Yell. Slam doors. *Something*.

Not this silence.

Arabella: *Owen? Please. We need to talk.*

Still nothing. He's done. That thought cracks something in me. His choice to ignore me, to completely lock me out—it makes me nauseous. I think of Ophelia, how sick she got when Julian was sent to Hell, closing their link. Would Owen let that happen to me?

He wouldn't.

Would he?

Because the Owen I knew—the one who used to catch me in the dark—feels far away. And maybe it's my fault. Maybe I pushed him too far. But right now? I don't know who I am anymore... I don't know anything anymore.

I cry a little more. Letting the emotions seep out of me. I need to let it all out. I cried for God knows how long.

"What the fuck were you thinking!" A voice says from the corner of the room.

I look up and see Ophelia standing there. Her eyes are ignited, there are literal flames where her irises were. She's fuming and has her target set on me. I've never been so terrified.

I play dumb. "What do you mean?"

"You know exactly what I mean, Arabella!" She screams. "You spoke out of turn. You *provoked The Council!*"

I don't even bother to stand. My voice almost neutral. "Oh my god. Not you too."

"You don't get to say that" she snaps, her voice is getting danger-ously low. "You don't get to act like the victim here, Arabella."

"I already got the riot act from Josie, okay?" I fire back. "She gave me the whole speech. About how I ruined everything, how I made it about me—trust me, I've heard it."

Ophelia stops short. "Josie?" she repeats. "Bella, I'm not here to echo Josie. I don't care what she said." She steps forward. "This isn't about how you looked in that room. It's about what you *cost* us."

My throat tightens. "I was trying to help—"

"In doing that, you took down everything we've been building." She shrieks again. "You didn't just get Owen cut off. You got our entire family exiled. We've been erased from the Council. Do you understand that? The Duvain name means nothing now."

She's trembling. Rage and something deeper—hurt.

I scoff, heat rushing up my spine. "*We?*" I snap. "You're really saying 'we' like you're one of them now?"

That does it. Ophelia goes scarily still.

Her voice drops to a lethal level. "One of *them*?"

She takes a step forward. "You think I'm defending *them*? After everything I've done—for you? For us?" The flames circling her pupils flare harder. "You don't get to question my loyalty when you're the one who destroyed the goddamn foundation. The family that took you in! Us in!"

I open my mouth. She's not done.

"Because of *you*, we're the laughingstock of the demon courts. Julian..." Her voice cracks. "My *soulmate* has to walk around pretending it doesn't gut him every time someone mocks our name. And you have the audacity to act like I've picked a side that *isn't yours?*"

She steps even closer, and I can feel the heat of her fury radiating off her skin.

"I've always been on your side, Arabella. Even when you didn't deserve it. Even when you made mistake after mistake and never looked back." Her voice breaks just slightly. "But I can't keep standing beside someone who keeps trying to be a martyr for the wrong cause. You're ruining lives in the process."

I make to try to interject again, but she doesn't give me the chance

"You didn't just hurt Owen. You humiliated Julian. You humiliated *me*. And for what? A moment where you got to feel like the hero?" She starts to turn, then hesitates. "You say Josie gave you the riot act. Fine. Let her. But don't you dare confuse *that* with what this is. This isn't a lecture."

She looks me dead in the eye. "This is me telling you—I don't know if I can ever trust you again."

She leaves before I can say anything. Portaling home, I assume.

I'm exhausted, I'm lost, I'm embarrassed. Not just for me, but for them.

What the fuck did I do?

I bury my hands in my hair and stare at the worn wooden floor. She was right. God she was so right it hurts to admit.

I've spent so long convincing myself I had to do it all alone. That no one else would fight hard enough.

All I've done is hurt people. The people who stood beside me. Who tried to *warn* me. I shoved them aside. Because I thought I had to be a one woman army.

But no one asked me to fight alone. I just didn't know how to let anyone *in*.

I just destroyed the only family I ever had. I need to fix it.

> I need help. You have some time?

Della

> Your place?

> Yeah. I'd ask how you know, but what's the point.

Della

Be there in 10.

Exactly ten minutes later, Della steps through a shimmering portal in the corner of my bedroom. The look on her face tells me everything. She already knows what happened. She's not going to coddle me. She is going to help me fix it.

"I can't take anyone else screaming at me today," I mutter. My voice is raw. My throat hurts. "I know I was wrong."

"Good," she says, calm as ever. She crosses her arms and cocks an eyebrow. "Glad you know. Let's fix it."

"I can't," I say, shaking my head and turning away from her. I wish it was enough to hide myself from her, from everything.

"You *can*. But the real question is—are you finally ready to listen to someone else?" she says. She grabs my arm and tightens her grip, just slightly. She isn't trying to hurt me. She's just trying to help me.

I wince, but keep my mouth shut. Time to eat some humble pie. She watches me for a moment longer before smirking.

"Okay you're ready," she laughs.

I don't get a moment to ask what she means. She claps her hands once and lifts me to my feet. "Up you go. We have somewhere to be."

"Where?" I ask, standing up with her help.

"To the Council," she says. "To beg your way back into good standing. For the Duvains. They'll meet with *me*. Besides..." Her eyes narrow slightly. "You need to take your punishment."

If I have to crawl back to fix this, I will.

My family means everything to me.

This is *mine* to answer for.

I started this... Now I have to finish it. Before it's too late.

Chapter Sixteen
Owen

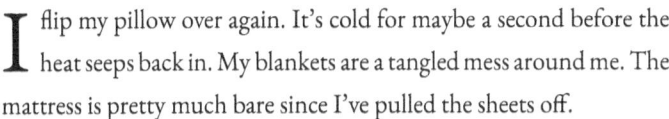

I flip my pillow over again. It's cold for maybe a second before the heat seeps back in. My blankets are a tangled mess around me. The mattress is pretty much bare since I've pulled the sheets off.

I don't regret what I said to Bella. Not really anyway.

But every time I close my eyes, I hear her voice floating through my mind. She sounds wrecked. Begging me to answer her.

What did I do? I slammed that door shut and locked it tight. I blocked her out. Of my mind, our communication, and our bond.

I groan and flip onto my back, staring at the ceiling. I clench my jaw so tight that it starts to ache.

Stubborn woman I think to myself. Then again, maybe I'm not any better.

Too stubborn to hear her out. To listen to an apology.

I think about the fallout. Everything that happened with the council. What my family said. How they must be feeling. Fuck even the look on Bella's face—it all plays on a constant loop in my head.

I know she was trying to help. But why couldn't she have just trusted me!

I press the heel of my hand to my eyes.

Why the fuck did I do that?

I said I needed space. But it wasn't space that I needed. It was punishment. I wanted her to feel what I felt when everything was taken from me.

We were supposed to go in there as a team. Fight together. She wanted to do everything herself.

That is the root of it. It's not about her wanting me or loving me for that matter.

I want her to need me. To never feel like she's going to war alone.

Not as a savior. More like a constant. My person that can shut down everything negative in my life and turn it positive with a smile.

I throw the covers off.. I don't care. I can't sleep. Why do I even bother?

I conjure some clothes with a thought, at least we still have that ability. The last thing I expected to see when I walked to my living room was a group of people.

I freeze in the doorway, greeted by my mother, aunt, father and uncle.

"What are you doing here?" I ask. I'm not angry that they're here. I'm just tired.

"Julian was worried." My father crosses his arms and leans against the fireplace. "He told us to come talk to you."

"He told us about what Bella did." My mother walks over to me. "We understand your anger, son. But your mark is dim."

My brows furrow in confusion until I look down and want to be sick. She's right, the mark on my forearm is dim. Somehow, less than a day after a fight, it started to lose it's flare.

"How is it dimming this fast?" I ask, eyes wide as I meet her gaze. "Julian and Ophelia's bond wasn't like this when they were separated."

"You blocked her out, Owen," Theron says, tone bone-dry. "Ah yes. Severing a fated bond always ends *so* well." I really don't need his sarcasm right now.

"I'm fine," I say, my resolve settling in, I square my shoulders again. "You don't need to worry about me."

"You don't look fine," Selene says with a snort.

"Duvain men are always stubborn. It's a miracle our mates tolerate us at all," Theron quips.

"Theron," my father grumbles out.

"What? It's true." Theron shrugs like it isn't a big deal.

"If I unblocked her…" I clear my throat. "Would that make a difference? Fix anything?"

"It would let her feel you again. She would know that you're willing to listen. Talk about it," my mother says. She walks towards me and puts her hand on my shoulder.

"Her choice was reckless, but yours was cruel," Selene adds.

"I just—" I run my hand through my hair. "I was angry! And worried! The council took everything from us. My ability to make contracts. Our family's connection to them. Our standing in the community."

Theron scoffs, shifting my attention to him. "We've held that Accord together longer than half those demons have drawn breath."

"If they want to revoke favors and throw tantrums… Let them. We don't grovel. We'll just adapt," my mother adds.

"She didn't mean for this outcome. I know this. When I cut her off, I made her think that I stopped believing in her. That's on me," I sigh.

"She needs to feel you. Open your link. She needs to know you're still hers. That you'll let her be wrong and still love her through it," Selene says, sitting on my couch.

"Duvains don't exile our own. We rebuild... and we do it together," my mother says.

"I have to go," I say making for the door. "I have to find her."

I open the link, but I don't feel her. It's like she's gone, I can't even sense her emotions.

Owen: *Bella... I'm sorry. Please reach out. Please*

I wait another minute pacing the room. Nothing at all.

"She's not responding," I say.

"Well sense her and go to her, son," my father says like it's the easiest thing in the world.

"I can't sense her either," I say, starting to panic.

I don't wait for a response. I'm already gone—headed straight to Hearthlight.

Josie is the one who answers my insistent pounding on the door, pulling her headphones out of her ears.

"Owen..." She trails off surprised.

"Where is she?" I ask, searching the apartment like a crazed man. "I need to talk to her."

"I don't know," Josie replies confused, blinking at me. "I'm just about to go to work."

"Wait...You weren't with her last night?" I ask, stopping short and staring at her with confusion that I know is clear on my face.

"No," she says slowly, like it should be obvious that she wasn't there last night. "I was spending the night with my boyfriend."

She turns and grabs her coat and bag on the couch. "I'll check her office," she says, rushing towards the door. "Maybe she went in early."

"I'm going with you," I say.

"Wouldn't expect otherwise," she says, chuckling. She doesn't seem worried, that's a good sign, right?

We step into the hall and I bounce my foot as I watch her lock the door. I don't think I've ever felt anxiety like this in my life. I need to get to her more than I need my next breath.

"You really don't know where she went?" She asks while we walk to the center of Hearthlight, chewing on her bottom lip.

I shake my head. "We haven't spoken since the...incident." I wince at the phrase, but I can't think of anything else to say when we might be overheard."

Josie's brow lifts, it's the only indication of her surprise. "That's not like her."

"No," I whisper. "It's not."

We walk to Bella's office and I see her door is open, but she's not in it.

"Owen," Emery says, startled. "What are you doing here?"

"Looking for Bella," I say. I may have snapped at her a little too hard, but I can't find it in myself to care at the moment. I'm desperate to find my soulmate.

"That's weird..." She trails off.

"Why?" I ask, snapping my attention to her face.

"We assumed she was with you," she says, chewing on her lip in concern or confusion, I'm not sure which.

"We?" I raise a brow.

"Yeah. I just talked to Tinsley about what her to do list is," she says. "Here's yours, Josie."

Josie takes the list and reads over it.

"This sounds like parts of Bella's job," she says, looking at me worried.

"I got licensed as a Social Worker so my note says I'm interim director until she returns," Emery says, nodding.

"Until she returns?" I parrot, trying not to let the panic set in. She could be anywhere. Why didn't she tell me? What if someone took her? What if it was Rhys? I can't stay here.

"That's what Della said when she brought this to me," Emery says, yanking my attention back to the present moment and out of the 'what if' spiral.

"I think I need to have a conversation with Della," I mutter, opening a portal without another word.

Something is very wrong. I have a bad feeling about this. Worse than being shut out. I can't *sense* her. That only happens when the mate is...*don't go there Owen.*

Taking a breath, I walk into Hex & Brews and see Della at the counter. She locks eyes with me. There is something in her gaze that leaves me on edge. She tries to hide it immediately, but it's too late.That's all I need to see—I stride straight up to the counter.

"We need to talk," I say, not giving her any room to argue.

She nods her head and follows me to the back.

We step into her card room. This is where she does all of her readings in the store. It's so Della. Muted colors and all. I can smell the incense and I feel like I'm wrapped in a hug.

She gestures to the two chairs across from each other, velvet and worn at the edges. Timeless and lived in.

Thankfully, I don't have to tell her that we need privacy, she's already locking the door by the time I turn around.

Though this looks like a regular reading room, I know better. Della is powerful. I don't know where she keeps her legitimate magical materials, but I can only guess it's in an attic somewhere.

"I know why you're here," she says, her voice calm, bracing.

"Tell me where she is," I say.

"Why do you think I know where she is?" She asks.

"Don't play coy with me, Della," I say, standing up and starting to pace back and forth. "She gave *you* a list of instructions to give to Tinsley, Emery, and Josie. She would never just up and leave! How would you not know where she went?"

"Why do *you* care?" She asks, crossing her arms.

"Excuse me?" I raise my brow, voice deceptively soft. I don't enjoy being questioned.

"You heard me," she says. She is clearly not backing down. Not until I admit it anyway.

"Yes. I did," I say.

"So answer," she says. Her voice turns cold as she repeats herself. *"Why do you care?"*

"Because..." I say. "She is my mate and I love her."

"You see, that isn't enough," she says, tapping her foot on the ground. Her voice might be neutral, but her eyes tell me everything. She's pissed and has no right to be. "You shut her out. Locked her out from *her* soulmate. You made her believe that she'd been abandoned."

I try to speak, but she holds her hand up.

"Let me finish." She steps closer to me. "I'm not saying you shouldn't have been angry. Or that she should have done what she did. She was wrong, there's no doubt about that. But you didn't help. You put her at risk."

"A lecture, Della," I say, rolling my eyes. "Really?"

"You *both* needed one apparently," she says, her eyes flash with a motherly anger, like we're her children that she's about to punish.

"She just fought for why she was right instead of listening," I say. "She could've apologized."

"She *did* try to apologize, Owen," she says. "She sent a message. She waited. Sent another one and waited. You chose to block the connection and she took your silence as an answer."

"She always wants to take charge to do things," I say.

"Since you decided to not hear her, she felt like she *had* to do it herself," she says. "She was stubborn. She was righteous, as you say. So damn convinced she was right she couldn't look ahead to see what could happen."

I stay silent, speechless. I have nothing that I can say back because she's right.

I shift from foot to foot. "So, where did she go?"

"She went to the council."

I freeze, staring at Della slack jawed. "How did she even get there?"

"I took her," she says. "She needed to fix this. Someone had to take the step in fixing what you both broke."

"She went in? And what? Begged?" I ask in disbelief.

"No," she says. "She stood in front of them. Offered whatever punishment they decided to give her. All for your family—and for your name."

I tighten my jaw. "Is Bella okay?"

"Your family is back in good graces with the council. Ophelia's Loom has been returned," she says. "As for your bond, it will return when Bella does."

She completely ignores my question. But she said when she returns, so that means she's going to come back. I'll have my mate back

My face must say it all because she says, "You are tied to each other being mates and all. Once she is finished learning her lesson, your punishment will end as well."

"My punishment?" I ask. *The council is punishing me? For what? I tried to stop her.*

"They knew the minute you severed your connection with her," she says. "You abandoned your mate, so your punishment is sitting with not knowing where she is."

She turns around and walks out of the room without another word.

I blow out a breath and sit down in one of the chairs. *What the fuck?*

She still has the tarot cards laid out. I thought it was for someone else, but when I look, I can't help it... I laugh.

These cards were meant for me. She always knew I was coming.

The Tower. The Hanged Man. Judgement.

Of course. The fallout, the consequences, and what I need to change or atone.

Oh, Bella.

Not the Bella who screamed at the council. The Bella who took a chance on us. She was married and still believed in the bond. The one who'd believe I'd find a way, even when I didn't. The one who begged me to listen.

I didn't listen.

I think about the way her voice sounded through the bond before I did what I did—tight, cracking around the edges, desperate to reach me. I can't unhear it now. I can't forgive myself for it either.

I clench my fists at my sides, trying to breathe. Trying to not feel it. But it's there—buzzing under my skin. The bond.

Twisting. Suffocating.

Her voice shreds through my head. I put my hands to my head and squeeze as I let out a guttural scream. I can't stop the noise. Her voice. The pain.

The bond flares open and bursts at the seams.

I feel despair seeping around the edges of my soul. She's gone.

Well and truly gone.

She never wanted to be a hero. Not in the way people think. She just wanted to save people because she never really had a chance to save herself.

She has always been too much. I love that about her. All that passion in a person.

Why did I do this? Make her carry this punishment alone? I told her that she was a martyr. Doing everything alone over trusting me. Working with me. But I did just that to her. *Made* her do it alone.

My hands shake as I tear at the mark on my forearm, nails digging in until the skin splits open. The sting doesn't register at all. I want to feel something—anything—besides this hollow pit inside of me where Bella used to reside.

I failed her.

I keep clawing at my mark... no. *Our* mark. I just keep going until it's nearly unrecognizable. It starts to hurt almost enough to compare to what is inside of my chest.

A portal opens in front of me. My brothers and cousins all exist at once. Della must have called them. I don't know. I also don't care.

Julian puts his hand on my shoulder. He knows what I'm going through. He's been through it before.

"What do I do?" I ask him.

"You fight," he says. "And you be there for her when she gets back because something tells me she will never be the same again."

Chapter Seventeen
Arabella

Della and I appear in front of the Infernal Palace. It looks different than last time. Or maybe it's me that's different.

Everything changes when the agenda is less about fighting and more about groveling.

"I can't go in with you," Della says in a sympathetic tone. "I already arranged for the meeting. They're expecting you."

I sigh, a shiver running down my spine. I should've known this is my problem to fix.

"Okay," I say. "Here goes nothing."

I turn away from her and walk into the building. The doors are closed. Bone and obsidian glow when I touch them. They only open if the person who called the meeting arrives. Della called this session—for me.

Once they open, I'm greeted by the council. They are never here first. Or that's what Owen always said.

They're faces are the same as they were last time—voids, like black holes wrapped in velvet robes. Today feels unsettling. They feel... aware. No faces means no eyes. It's like the dark is watching back. I understand why people fear them now.

I am here to do the right thing. I see the rune on the floor. Already glowing. Waiting for me. So I walk to it. Stand on it, but wait for the council to say something first. I'm playing by their rules this time.

"This audience was granted by Della Sage," they say. "We are only here to honor that request."

I bow my head to them, but stay silent.

"Yet here is the girl who spat on our judgement before a solution could be rendered," they continue on. "Have you come to repeat your accusations? Or dig the Duvain family a deeper grave."

I decide to just let them speak until I am allowed to because my mouth is what got me in trouble the last time. I believe the council is starting to understand that I'm trying.

"You may speak, Arabella Arden," they say.

"I came to make amends," I say, standing tall, ignoring the sting of the. sound of my last name, my *father's* last name.

I don't ask for anything. I just speak from the heart. What I should've done that day, but didn't.

"That day—I didn't care what your laws were. I didn't care what anything was. My own agenda was more important than listening and responding. I saw injustice, and I exploded, reacted instead of listening." I just go with it. I shift uncomfortably.

"I accused you of cowardice when, the whole time, I was projecting my own insecurities. I never wanted to believe that the balance of nature would cost this much. I only thought of the one person and not the many," I continue.

"You name yourself the coward. Which you are correct in saying," they start. "You mistook silence for apathy. Power for neglect. You saw pain and presumed injustice. That is mortal arrogance. But also...mortal grief."

I nod, tears forming in my eyes. I tip my chin down to hide the fact that I want to cry. I don't want to show them yet another mortal weakness. The last thing that i want them to think is that I'm trying to gain sympathy or a lighter sentence. I know that I need to own up and take whatever it is that they'll throw at me, I'm just hoping that it won't be anything too...lasting.

"We do not move for suffering. We move for sacrifice. Not all things broken are unjust. Not all things grieved are wrong," they say.

"I understand that now," I say.

"You did not before," they say. It's not a question. It's a statement. They know the answer. "Pain clouds purpose."

"It does and for that, I am sorry," I say. "I was reckless. Righteous. And full of greed."

"You're here not just to apologize," they say.

"No. I want the Duvain family forgiven for my mistakes," I say. "They don't deserve this. Especially Owen."

"Then you must sacrifice," they say.

"I'll do anything." I bow slightly, I'm not sure if I'm supposed to or not, but it just feels right. Oh well, there's going back now.

"You will witness. And you will not speak. You will not interfere. You will witness," they say.

"Witness what?" I ask.

"The breaking of a soul."

I gasp and take a step back. *Holy shit.* This is not what I was expecting them to say at all.

"For two weeks, you will share his cell. You will watch the demon who is in charge of torturing focusing on him. As greed claws from the depths. You will follow the demon to watch the souls of once good people break," they say.

"Who?" I ask.

"You will meet the demon later, but the person is Cassius."

Well fuck! Cassius was not who I thought. I never expected to see my father again. Not since Ophelia sent him to Hell.

"Okay," I say, taking a shaky breath. "I'm willing to do this." *I can do this.* Yeah, the guy is a piece of shit, but he's still my father.

"It starts now," they say.

"Can I give a message to Della for Hearthlight?" I ask.

"Yes," they say in unison.

I leave the courtroom and see Della just standing outside the door.

"Hey," I know my voice gives away my nerves.

"What happened?" she asks, her voice muted. There's an edge to it, like she's bracing for the worst but hoping she's wrong.

"They gave me my sacrifice. I'll be gone for a couple of weeks," I say. I don't know how much time I have so I don't let her speak. "I need you to give Josie, Tinsley, and Emery some information about how to run Hearthlight in my absence. Emery is a Social Worker now so she can take over that end."

I spend the next few minutes with her writing down everything that needs to be done. Turns out Della keeps everything in her bag, including pen and paper.

The doors swing open revealing the council. "It is time."

I give Della a hug and walk into the courtroom. As the doors close, I turn to her.

"Tell Owen I'll be back soon. That everything is fixed and he will be when I get back, but don't tell him where I'm going. He can't go searching for me," I say.

"I will, Bella. I'll be here when you're done," she says. The doors shut all the way, effectively sealing me in.

"You will walk through the fire. The demon will meet you on the other side. Safe travels and good luck, Arabella Arden," they say.

The flames pull the moisture right from my skin—dry without heat. Like standing too close to a sun that shouldn't exist. My lips feel cracked by the time I pass through, but I don't dare lick them. The flames might taste regret.

It's a dark hallway. I was expecting screaming or skulls, but no. There aren't mounted trophies. It's just a long hallway with thousands of doors. There is no way that you could count them. It's never ending.

The flames close behind me. I'm stuck. Alone. Also terrified. This is the part of Hell I've never seen before, a part I never wanted to see, truth be told.

A door on my left opens and out walks one of the last people I thought I would see.

Damian Duvain. Owen's cousin.

"Damian?" I ask.

"You arrived faster than I anticipated, Bella" he says, tone as even as it is unreadable. "I'm the demon you'll be learning from."

"You?" I ask.

"The council called and I answered. It's a good thing they picked someone you know. Others might not be as caring," he says. "Come on. Cassius is this way."

There's something to be said for small mercies, I suppose.

I follow him down the hall. It feels like it's moving, yet we're staying the same. Still no screams.

"I thought it would be...louder," I say.

"Most do, but a large part of the torture is silence. No one likes when there is no noise. Their screams are always muffled," he says. "You'll spend the first week in Cassius' cell. Comforts have been added. You will stay with him, leave with him, witness his torture for the day and return."

"And the second week?" I ask.

"You'll stay in the dormitories with the handlers. For the week, I will stay with you. Adrian has been sworn to secrecy so he will not say that I am not home to anyone," he says.

"Okay," I say, trying to shake off my anxiety.

I follow Damian to a door with runes etched and carved into it's dark wooden surface.

He presses his palm to the metal and the markings flare—crawling up his arm like veins of light before the door clicks open.

"You'll begin here," Damian says, gesturing toward the chamber with a movement so minimal it's almost impersonal. "Cassius."

His voice is the first thing that hits me.

It's not the kind of voice that demands attention—it assumes it. Each word is cut clean, like glass dragged across marble. No wasted syllables. No filler. Just intent.

He speaks the way executioners swing swords—deliberate, quiet, with no ceremony.

"You'll observe," he continues. "Spend the night in his cell. Tomorrow, we begin again."

There's no anger in it. He watches me for a long moment, expression flat—like he's waiting for my fear to catch up to my understanding.

Damian steps inside, and I follow him, crossing the threshold.

I shiver. It feels real now.

Not just a sentence or a punishment spoken in cold voices, but reality.

The moment I step past the doorway, it's like something seals behind me. Like the world I knew has been locked away and this is all that's left.

My skin prickles, nerves taut. I swallow hard. Because this isn't about fear.

This is about surrendering to it. Learning from it. Paying what I owe.

My breath catches at the sight in front of me. Chains hang from the black hole that looks to be the ceiling, connecting to Cassius, holding him up.

He doesn't look like the man I knew. Not even close. Nothing like the father that I grew up seeing every day.

Yeah he sucked as a father. Worse than sucked. He was a bastard that deserves every minute of this. I had it bad, but Ophelia had it ten times worse.

But thinking about him being here and seeing it are two separate things. His hair is matted with sweat and blood. His jawline gaunt. None of the luxuries I'm used to seeing on him.

His eyes—once full of charm—are dull and glassy. He looks like he's going mad.

"Funny to see you here, daughter of mine," Cassius chuckles. "What did you do to end up in such a fine place?"

I just look at him, staying neutral. He doesn't need to know how much he affects me.

"Ophelia send you here too? Since you're with my handler here... you must be a Duvain," he says, cackling.

I show him my mark. I'm not ashamed of it. I'm proud.

"Ah I see. They want you to watch me after the fall. Well here I am, sweetheart!" He shouts.

Damian walks to the chains, cool and unfazed. "This is not theatre, Cassius. She is not your audience."

Damian turns and without a word, lifts his hand.

A black stone table rises from the obsidian floor encased in smoke. Instruments begin to appear on it.

Row by row. Column by column. It looks like hundreds of them. They aren't normal weapons like knives or guns. No, they're wrapped in runes and bend at the hilt. Some look scalpel adjacent and others like weird orbs.

On the other side of the room, a smoke screen appears. Like he is going to watch something.

"You'll sit over there," Damian says.

A chair pushes out from the wall. Silently, I go over and sit in it, getting a front row seat of what is going to happen to Cassius. There's absolutely no chance I'm messing this up. They told me to watch, not speak. So, that's exactly what I'm going to do.

My hands tighten against the armrest as everything begins.

The screen shifts.

Cassius's life unfolds in flickers of cold silver light. Young Cassius flashes first—the golden child. A clever boy with quick eyes and a quicker tongue, always knowing just how to twist a moment in his favor.

Adulthood plays like a stage performance. Power. Prestige. A trail of promises lined with broken bodies.

Next is a woman.

She appears in her mid twenties, with soft eyes and dark hair that falls to her shoulders in gentle waves. Her name isn't spoken, but the grief etched across her face says enough. She reaches out, trembling.

Before she turns to ash.

Not fire—ash. Disintegrating right in Cassius's arms as he screams in soundless horror.

I glance at Damian, confused.

Before I can speak, Cassius gurgles through a throat raw with silence. "That's your other sister, Arabella," he says. "The one Ophelia murdered."

I don't say a word.

If Ophelia did, there was a reason.

Damian's gaze flickers toward me. His expression doesn't change, but I feel it—the faint shift in his posture. He expected resistance. Outrage. A demand for answers.

He doesn't get one. The things he must have heard about me. About my big mouth.

The screen fades. Then come the tools.

Damian doesn't start with Cassius's body. He goes for the temples.

The first touch sends a flicker through Cassius's face. A wince. A twitch. But it's not pain—it's remembrance.

Each stroke of the blade lights up a different failure, a different face, a different moment when he chose himself over someone else.

He gasps. Jerks. Not from agony—but from clarity.

Because this is worse than torture.

This is truth.

He tries to speak. Damian doesn't let him. Not tonight.

I sit perfectly still in my chair. I don't look away.

And I don't feel bad.

If that makes me evil, so be it.

Because this isn't cruelty. *This* is justice.

Damian steps away from the table without a word. He doesn't look at Cassius. Doesn't speak to me. He simply turns and walks to a side door, pressing his palm against the infernal seal carved into the stone.

It clicks open with a hiss.

I know it's been hours since we walked in here. I don't know how I know, I just do.

"This way," he says.

My limbs ache from sitting still, but I don't complain. I follow him through a narrow hall lit by violet flame.

Another door. Another rune.

Damian opens it and gestures inside.

The room is split in two.

On the far side is where Cassius is. Still shackled. Still bleeding. Chained to the floor with no bed, no blanket, no water. Just stone.

The side—my side—is elevated by three steps and sectioned off by a transparent barrier humming with magic. As I pass, I press my fingers against it. The air is lighter here, warmer maybe.

My cot is small, but padded and plush, as comfortable as possible in a place like this. There's a steaming pile of food waiting on the bedside table with a napkin that matches the soft blanket and pillow case. Even the water sitting in the pitcher glows with magic. The juxtaposition is striking.

Cassius shifts on the floor below, coughing.

He tries to sit up straighter but the chains dig in. His eyes lift toward me, rimmed red and raw.

"I guess they gave you the suite," he mutters, voice cracking.

A cruel smile ghosts across his mouth, but it doesn't reach his eyes. He glances toward the magical barrier, testing it with his gaze.

"Don't worry," he adds. "They made sure I can't touch you. Wouldn't want the spoiled observer to get too close to the rot."

I don't say anything.

Damian doesn't wait for more. He turns and leaves, sealing the door behind him. The barrier between us flickers once—confirming what we both already know.

Cassius can't reach me. I won't reach for him.

A week goes by.

Seven days of my cot in a cell and meals that taste like nothing. Seven days of watching Damian try to break Cassius down.

Now, I'm ready to move on from Cassius.

Not because I forgive him. Not because I hate him. But because there's nothing left to watch.

The man I knew—the manipulator in gold, the strategist behind a hundred betrayals—he's gone.

What remains is a husk with too much knowledge and not enough hope. I no longer need to sit in the dark just to prove I see him clearly.

The door to the cell opens and Damian comes in.

"Cassius," he says, voice as flat and final as it was when he greeted me. "Say goodbye to Bella."

He glances back at me. This time, his eyes narrow just slightly. "Hopefully forever."

He just grunts and stands, not even sparing me a glance.

"Yeah whatever. Didn't want her in my life when I was alive, sure as shit don't want it now," he says, though his voice is flatter now than it was when I first entered.

He leaves to go to his punishment room and Damian leads me down a spiraling corridor, the walls narrowing as we descend.

We reach a set of massive double doors carved with layered runes. They pulse a faint onyx color, like a heartbeat beneath stone.

He presses a palm to the center. The doors unlock with a low, grinding hum.

The handler's dormitory is not a room. It's a cathedral.

The ceiling stretches impossibly high, vanishing into darkness. Stone arches rise overhead like skeletal wings. The walls are lined with relics—scenes of balance and punishment, carved in bone colored marble. No two are the same.

He stops at the third door on the left.

"This one's yours."

He doesn't linger.

The moment I touch the rune beside the handle, it pulses once. It's like it recognizes me.

The door clicks open.

The room is compact but self contained.

Stone walls, yes—but smoother here. Treated. Someone tried to make it... livable. Like that matters.

To the right is a narrow bed with charcoal sheets tucked tight, one black pillow, and a folded blanket at the foot. Everything in its place. Every corner is sharp. Controlled.

It reminds me of the handlers. How they moved. How they cleaned their blades after every session.

Across from it is a built-in desk with a drawer. The wardrobe is matte black. Inside hangs one uniform in grey.

To the left is a small door that leads to the private bathroom. Stone tile, a pressure controlled shower, and a steel sink with a mirrored panel above it that doesn't reflect the soul. Only the surface.

"Your shift starts in an hour. Change into your uniform," Damian says. "You're a low level handler so you will spend the next week following me and setting everything up."

Damian meets me at the handler corridor entrance an hour later.

The uniform is already on. The material clings like a second skin, designed for ease of movement—but there's no comfort in it.

Owen's name crossed my mind once.

Just once.

It hurts too much to stay in that frame of mind. I miss him with the same desperation as Ophelia missed Julian. The yearning and the agony.

Thinking of him makes everything worse.

Thinking of Hearthlight brings even more pain.

So, I don't.

I follow Damian without a word. "You're assigned to Chamber Five today," he says, not looking at me. "Prep and clean. You'll observe the session. Nothing more."

I nod. There's no room for questions here. No one cares if I'm ready.

The chamber is cold.

Sterile stone. Steel fixtures. A raised center platform with a single restraint chair—charred from use but still gleaming. Overhead, the soul mirror pulses faintly, waiting to reflect back what it's told to show.

I wheel in the prep cart.

I sweep the floor for any residual memory echoes, clean blood from the seams in the arm cuffs, place the extractor runes in their designated triangle around the base, and light the flame of truth.

When Damian enters with the soul, I step back into the corner.

I'm invisible. That's the point.

The soul screams for the first ten minutes. Not in pain. Just fear. Pleading. Rambling.

Damian doesn't flinch. He uses a memory siphon—draws out a moment and places it in the mirror. The man watches himself betray his own son.

He begs for it to stop.

It doesn't.

I don't look away.

Hours later the session ends. The man is dragged out sobbing uncontrollably.

I move forward again.

No hesitation. Blood. Slime. Burned threads of memory left behind like singed hair.

I clean it all. Wipe down the chair. Reset the runes. Reseal the
mirror. Refill the salt line.

Damian doesn't thank me. He just leaves.

That's how the rest of the week goes.

Prep. Watch. Clean.

The souls change. The pain doesn't.

By the seventh day, I know what I need to do.

I walk the halls with the other handlers, boots echoing in sync. I
speak only when required. I sleep without dreaming. And when a soul
looks at me, I don't look back.

I'm not here to punish. I'm here to see the importance of balance.
It's a machine. Not about one person. That's how the world works.
The symmetry in consequence.

Damian doesn't say anything when he arrives at my door. He just
waits, arms crossed, as I fold my uniform and place it in the trunk. I
don't take anything with me. I don't want to.

We walk through the stone halls. Up the soul slick stairs. Past the
the judgment and the ones who still think this is about fairness. Before
I see it.

A gate. A shimmer in the wall opens into a seam of cool grey light.

He steps forward, touching the runes. They part. Without ceremony, we walk through.

When I open my eyes again, we're outside my apartment.

Earth air hits differently, it smells like rain. The overcast sky and the
freshness of the air should feel like a relief, it should make me smile,
but it doesn't feel real.

Damian exhales through his nose and nods toward my door.
"You're done," he says.

Unexpectedly, he steps forward and pulls me into a hug. It's brief and awkward, like he isn't sure how exactly to perform the gesture.

"If you hadn't made that sacrifice," he says, voice low, "our family wouldn't have its name back."

He lets go and disappears before I can answer.

I stare at the door for a full thirty seconds before I open it.

I step inside and stop. They're all here.

Owen is closest, pacing near the door with a crease between his brows. He freezes the second he sees me.

Emery's on the arm of the couch, fidgeting with his ring. Della sits cross legged beside him. Josie's in the corner with a cup of tea she hasn't touched. Ophelia and Julian stand side by side near the window.

Tinsley's tucked beside Julia on the far end of the sectional—curled up, blinking at me like I stepped out of a dream.

The room goes still.

No one speaks.

Owen moves. His long legs eating up the space between us.

"I'm okay," I whisper, forcing the sound out hurts my throat. I hadn't realized just how long it's been since I've spoken anything out loud.

He pulls me into his arms, practically crushing me with his strength. He's trying to anchor me to this plane. Like if he holds me tight enough, no one can take me away again.

He kisses me. Deep. Desperate in a way only he knows how to hide.

The kind of kiss that says *you're real. You're here. You're mine.*

Chapter Eighteen
Arabella

"Where the *fuck* were you?" Owen asks, growling.

I look around the room. Everyone who loves me is sitting there. Della is the only one who knows what happened—some of where I was.

The others want to. I see it on their faces. The questions. The worry. The fear that something broke in me.

I shake my head. "Can we talk about it later?" My voice is more of a croak than anything else, I wince at the sound. "I want to rest."

"Of course," he says, his voice softening. the look on his face is heartbreaking, I'm not sure what to make of it right now.

I walk toward the bedroom and see Josie's suitcase stuffed into my closet. But my bed is made.

Exactly how I do it. I always make my bed with the hospital style folds and the pillow turned down just a bit.

Josie must be sleeping on the pullout.

I go into my closet, pull out some leggings and a sweater. I want to shower and to wear something familiar considering the grey uniform I wore for a week.

Pulling them on, I crawl into bed and wrap myself in the blankets.

I don't know how long I'm crying for. Eventually I feel Owen come up behind me. He slips in the bed, his body heat encircling me and warming me to my core. He pulls me into his arms.

"I've got you, Belladonna," he whispers into my hair. "Cry it out."

For a week I'm like this. A whole week I feel withdrawn.

I go through the normal motions—eat a little, sleep a lot, sit on the couch while everyone around me talks.

"Enough," Della says. "Bella, it's time to talk. Snap out of it."

Little did she know that I was thinking the same thing.

"I agree. I think it's time I tell all of you what happened those two weeks I was gone," I sigh.

"Two weeks?" Josie asks.

"Yeah," I say, preparing myself to open up and be vulnerable.

"Baby, you were gone for over a month," Owen says, his brow furrowed.

"Over a month!" I exclaim. "The council said two weeks!"

"Were you in Hell?" Julian asks, tilting his head in curiosity.

"Yeah, I was," I say, I thought that would have been obvious.

"That makes sense," he says.

"How?" I ask.

"Time works differently in Hell, Belladonna," Owen says gently, grabbing my hand and brushing his thumb along the top of it. "What happened when you were there?"

I sit forward on the couch. My palms start to sweat when I think about my time there. I'm not scared or nervous to tell them. It's not like I don't want to relive it. A lot transpired down there.

"I don't even know where to start," I admit. "It was a lot to say the least."

They all wait for me to gather myself. No one rushes me. They're there for support.

"I went to Hell by choice. I sought out the Council. Della got a meeting with them for me," I start. "I wanted to apologize, but I really wanted to understand why they wouldn't help Tinsley. Save the innocent."

Owen nods at me to continue.

"They didn't do anything bad. They didn't torture me," I say. "They did make me see. I shared a cell with Cassius for a week. I watched him be punished. And I couldn't do or say anything."

"You saw Cassius? Julian, I need to talk to the council. They should have never—" Ophelia starts.

"Quiet, Ophelia. Let Bella talk," Della cuts in.

Ophelia wants to retort, I can see it in her face. But Julian pulls her into his arms and gives her a sharp shake of his head.

"If you can't control yourself, then leave. Or stay silent and listen," Della snaps, more cold than I've ever heard her.

I never thought she'd be the one to stand up to Ophelia, but I'm thankful for it. I don't want to focus on Cassius.

"I spent the second week with the handlers in their dorm." I don't think it's my place to tell them who exactly I was with. That felt like something only he'd be able to tell them. "I shadowed a handler and I was his assistant for the week. I lived with them. Ate with them. Watched how they work. I realized that it's about order and balance, not cruelty. Eventually, once their soul is broken down enough for the horrible humans they were, they are released."

I swallow hard. It's like all of the memories are rushing toward me all at once. All the blood floats up to my head.

"I thought I could fight fate. That if I screamed loud enough or cared hard enough, it would change the rules. But love isn't enough if it ignores balance. I get that now."

Owen squeezes my hand.

"I'm not proud of everything I said down there," I finish. "But I'm glad I learned what I did. Because it changed me. I can still fight, but to keep the balance intact instead of destroying it."

"You should've told me," Ophelia says, her voice hoarse. "You could have told me you were going to the council."

I look at her. "You would've tried to stop me."

"Of course I would have!" She exclaims.

"I needed to own what I did, Ophelia."

Her eyes start to glint. "You always do that. Carry the world like no one else can help. You have to be the martyr for everyone else."

Della tilts her head slightly, the faintest knowing smile on her lips.

"You're not mad she went," she says casually. "You're mad she did it alone and didn't tell you about it."

"Yes, I'm mad she did it alone! She didn't say a word to me! She went to *you*," Ophelia says.

"Of course she went to me," Della says softly. "Because she knew I wouldn't try to stop her."

Ophelia blinks.

"She wasn't looking for permission," Della continues. "She was looking for someone who understood that this was something *she* had to do. Even if it hurt. Even if it scared the rest of us."

There's no malice in her voice. She's not trying to be mean. Just telling her the truth. Cold hard truth.

"And maybe she didn't tell you," she adds, "because she didn't want to see that look on your face. The one that says *don't go* when she already knew she had to."

She looks around at everyone.

"But hey," she adds with a small smile, "welcome to the Bella Goes Rogue club. It's exclusive, but we've got good snacks."

Laughter bubbles out. Even Ophelia cracks a smile, rubbing a hand over her face.

For a moment, everything feels like it used to. Until Owen clears his throat, that is.

"Who was the handler you were working with?" he asks deceptively soft.

My smile falters. I glance down.

"Bella," he says, placing a finger under my chin to force me to meet his eyes. "Who was it?"

I hesitate, chewing the inside of my cheek. He never told me not to tell anyone, but it was clear the council had told him to stay quiet. It feels wrong to say it, to tattle on him like he's the one who did something wrong. But looking into my mates eyes, seeing the love and concern there, I can't keep it from him.

"Damian," I finally say.

"My *cousin* Damian?" He asks, his eyes flashing red for a fraction of a heartbeat.

"The council assigned him to it," I rush out, trying to justify it.

"Yet he said nothing to anyone," he mutters. He's angry. No, he's fuming mad.

"We were all having dinner at mom's house too. He never said any-thing," Julian says, he's looking at his knuckles, almost nonchalantly.

"He couldn't," I say. "Everything was top secret."

He shakes his head. Anger is still prevalent.

"I think Bella and I need to talk," Owen says, his voice stretched thin, like holding in everything he wants to talk about until everyone is gone.

"I agree," I say. I get up and hug everyone, thanking them for caring so much about me. But it's time Owen and I hash some things out.

"Your house?" I ask Owen.

"Yeah, let's go home," he says, grabbing my hand.

Let's go home. He still loves me, still wants me in his space, still wants to be with me. the thoughts ground me, keep me stable.

We portal straight to his house. It looks completely different. Not in a way most people would be able to see. But, I notice it all right away.

Deep crimson throw pillows against the charcoal couch. A warm toned rug beneath the coffee table. A vase with fresh red blooms on the windowsill, like someone dared color into his monochrome world.

Even the walls have hints of red in the artwork. Like fire breaking through smoke.

"Red?" I ask softly, almost not believing it.

Owen steps behind me, his voice low. "It's your favorite color. I missed you. When I thought you weren't coming back, I had to find a way to keep you here."

My heart pulls tight. I glance around again. It's not just red.

It's the love that he put into it.

"Time to talk. About us," I say.

Owen doesn't say anything. He sits down next to me.

"I'll start," I whisper. "Because I have to."

I stare at my knees. At my hands. Anywhere but at him.

"I tore down what you built," I say. "I thought I was doing the right thing—fighting for someone who couldn't fight for themself. But I wasn't fighting for justice. I was fighting because I was angry. Because I wanted to *matter*. And I didn't think about what that would cost you."

The tears come quietly now.

"I wasn't just wrong. I was *cruel*. I didn't ask. I didn't *trust* you. I was so wrapped in what I believed that I forgot what you'd already sacrificed to stand beside me."

I choke back a sob and force myself to say it.

"I stood in front of the council and I called them cowards. Useless. I spat on everything you'd spent lifetimes building. I screamed like I was the only one who cared, like Tinsley was the only one with something to lose."

His jaw tenses, but he doesn't interrupt.

"I told them their justice was broken," I whisper. "And in doing that, I made sure *you* paid the price. I watched them rip your favor away. Your seal. Your name. And I didn't even beg them to stop. I was so consumed by my rage, I didn't even look at you."

My voice breaks.

"You bowed to them, Owen. You tried to protect me even then. I didn't stop. I doubled down. I made you kneel for me while I burned the bridge you built from ash and blood."

My fists curl in my lap.

"I wanted to matter. I wanted them to listen. But all I did was scream over the one person who's always stood up for me when it counted most."

I look at him now—really look. Eyes that watched me destroy his power with words that weren't even mine to say.

"But I never even asked what yours cost."

Tears stream down my face.

"I'm sorry, Owen. For the legacy I tore down. For the authority I mocked. For using your name like a weapon when all you ever did was try to protect me."

My voice trembles, but I keep going.

"That's why I went back," I say. "Why I asked them to punish me. It wasn't about me anymore. It was about you. Your name. Your family. Everything I took from you without even realizing the depth of it."

His eyes meet mine—wet, unreadable.

"Della asked them for an audience," I say. "Not to plead for mercy. To fix it. To make sure House Duvain still meant something. That everything was restored. That the favor you'd spent lifetimes earning wasn't burned away because I couldn't control my own righteousness."

I reach for his hand.

"They gave it back, Owen. All of it. The name. The seal. Your right to stand in front of them again."

Tears fall freely now, but I don't look away.

"I know it doesn't erase what I did. But I wanted you to have back what I destroyed. Because you should *never* have had to lose it for me."

"I wasn't angry at the council," he says quietly. "I wasn't angry because they took my seal. Or our favor. Or the name I spent lifetimes protecting."

He's looking at me, but he's not really seeing me. His gaze is far away. Inside.

"I was angry at you," he admits. His voice cracks. "Not because I hated you. God, never that. I don't think I could stop loving you if I tried."

My breath hitches.

"I was angry because you left me behind," he whispers. "Because you walked into that courtroom, said those things and never once thought about what could happen to me."

His hands clench in his lap.

"I felt betrayed. Not just as your partner. As your person. Like I wasn't worth bringing with you into the fight. Like I didn't matter when it really counted."

He takes a shaky breath.

"And I get it," he says. "You were angry. You were scared. You were trying to protect Tinsley. But I was there, Bella. I was *right there*. You chose to take the situation into your own hands instead of being there with me."

His voice goes low. Cracked and raw.

"I would've followed you. I would've stood beside you, even if it meant losing everything. But you didn't give me that choice. You threw me out of the story."

I can see how vulnerable he's being and how much he is struggling with it.

"So I threw you out too," he says. "I blocked you out. I told myself I was allowed to because it is all your fault this happened to begin with. But really... I was just trying not to feel how badly it hurt."

He finally looks at me. "Then Della told me you went back to face the council." His breath stutters. "You went back to fix what I never thought could be fixed. Not because I asked you to. Not because anyone told you to. But because you knew what it cost me. What it cost my family."

His voice drops to a whisper.

"I'm so sorry," he chokes. "For shutting you out. For making you think you weren't worth fighting beside. For letting my pride speak louder than my love."

His hands are in my hair now. On my back. Around my waist.

"I never stopped being yours," he breathes. "I just got too scared to show it."

My throat tightens. I reach for him, fingers brushing his jaw. His skin is warm, damp with tears neither of us are trying to hide anymore.

"I didn't feel you," I whisper. "When you shut me out... you were gone, Owen. I reached for you, and it was just empty."

His face crumples.

"But I still wanted you," I say, voice shaking. "Every minute. Every breath. Even when it hurt. Even when I was furious and broken and trying to hold everything together—I just wanted *you*."

He grips my wrist, his thumb pressing into my pulse like he needs proof I'm real.

"I think a part of me wanted to protect you. To make you more careful," he says. "I learned that I don't want that. I love you for who you are and I don't want to change that part of you. I just want us to do it together."

He leans forward slowly, pressing his forehead to mine.

"We're going to be okay," he says.

"I know," I breathe. "Because this time... we do it together."

He nods. And then he pulls me into his arms like he never intends to let go.

"Bella, I want to make this official," he says. "I want our soulmate bond to be complete. The infernal claim."

"I want to be yours, Owen. Officially. Fully. Forever."

"Let me claim you," he whispers.

"Claim me," I whisper back. "I'm yours."

His mouth crashes into mine.

He picks me up like I weigh nothing—like I belong in his arms—and carries me to the bedroom.

Then he drops me onto the mattress with a grin that's all predator and promise.

His lips find mine again as he slides up my body, slow and deliberate, every inch of him pressed to every inch of me.

His hands are everywhere—gripping, teasing, *learning* me all over again.

He's not just touching me.

He's claiming me.

"Want me to make you mine?" he growls, voice thick and wrecked.

I smirk, tugging him down by his shirt.

"Show me what you can do."

His eyes darken and his mouth curves into something sinful.

"Don't worry, Belladonna," he murmurs. "I'm going to ruin you beautifully."

Chapter Nineteen
Arabella

H is words. His voice. Everything about him is utter perfection. I'm ready for us to be one...officially anyway.

"I choose this," I say, and my voice doesn't shake. "Not because of fate. Not because of what we're told we're supposed to be. I choose you. Fully. Freely. I surrender who I was... to become what we are."

"You understand what your words mean?" he asks, being sure. His voice cracks at the edges. I wonder if he's a little nervous that I might take it back.

It's not just our lives as we know it on the line, but his heart too.

"Yes." I'm certain. I don't need to think harder. I don't need time. Just him.

"There's no taking it back." His thumb brushes over my cheek. His body is rock solid above me.

"I don't want to," I say, meaning every word.

The Mark doesn't wait.

The moment I choose him—truly choose him—it ignites beneath my skin, not with heat but with hunger. It tears open across my heart like a wound made by intention alone, black at the edges, thick and wet at the center, seeping with something darker than blood. It breathes like a mouth. It wants, it *desires*.

I gasp—but Owen's mouth is already there, catching the sound, swallowing it. His kiss is deep, demanding, meant to pin me to this moment. And it works. My body trembles, not from fear, but from the rush of something ancient waking inside me.

The pain blooms. Spreads. Licks down my spine in hot pulses.

He kisses me harder.

His hands find my waist, my ribs, my throat. Anchoring. Grounding. Worshiping and containing all at once.

The Mark throbs against my skin—alive now. It doesn't speak, but I feel its question. It demands no offering. But it opens a hollow inside me that only he can fill.

And I know what it wants.

Owen doesn't flinch. His arms tighten. His lips move against mine like he's chasing the pain, needing it, needing me in the same way.

My body turns inside out.

Nerves scream. Bones stretch and strain and crack like glass under pressure. My skin feels too tight. My blood feels wrong. My heartbeat stutters, then collapses, then starts again in a rhythm that doesn't feel like mine. In time with his.

I gasp against his mouth—but he doesn't stop. He won't stop. His presence keeps me tethered, even as everything else inside me shreds and reforms.

His hands claim my body like it's the only anchor he trusts to keep me here. His voice breaks against my skin, a whisper jagged with need. "Come back to me."

I don't answer with words. I pull him closer.

His lips find the Mark again, and this time when he kisses it, it responds. My back arches. My fingers dig into his shoulders. And for one perfect second, the pain recedes—just enough to let the love through.

He worships every part of me that shattered.

I love every piece of him that broke watching it happen.

"You're mine," I whisper, voice thick with everything I can't say.

"I've *always* been yours," he says, kissing the words into my mouth like a vow.

He thrusts into me in one motion. His body fits perfectly against mine. Like a key finally shoved into a lock that forgot what it was waiting for.

He moves again—slow at first, controlled, like he's afraid I'll get hurt if he gives in to what's really burning behind his eyes. But I don't want slow.

"Don't hold back," I moan.

His gaze darkens—amber swallowed by red. Something ancient peers through.

And then he gives in, completely and entirely.

His hips slam into mine sending sparks of agony-laced pleasure spiraling through me. The bond tightens like a vice, wrapping around every nerve ending, twisting, pulsing with each thrust.

The rhythm builds—wild, desperate, *consuming*.

I writhe beneath him, meeting every brutal drive with a cry that doesn't sound like me.

There's nothing gentle in how he takes me. He growls against my throat, lips dragging down to my Mark, tongue tracing the jagged edges of power still raw and throbbing.

"You feel this?" he rasps. "This is us."

Another thrust. Deeper. Harder.

"This is what it means to be *mine.*"

I scream his name. My nails rake down his back. He doesn't flinch.

His hand wraps around my throat—not tight, just expanding my pleasure even further. My walls tighten around him, slick and pulsing with heat and magic and love that tastes like blood and lightning.

My climax slams into me. My body convulses. My vision whiteouts. The bond explodes.

He fucks me through it—driving me higher, wrecking me all over again. His release hits with a roar, his whole body shuddering as he empties into me, fingers bruising my hips, mouth crushed to mine.

He collapses against me, his body a shuddering weight, his breath hot and ragged against my throat.

Neither of us speak.

Our bodies are still locked together, skin slick, blood drying in strange places, the Mark on my chest throbbing at the same rhythm as the beat of our hearts.

Our hearts,, because they're now beating in unison.

His lips brush my collarbone. I wrap my legs tighter around his waist, not letting him pull away.

Owen rolls off of me and onto the bed. He's still panting.

Without a word, he pulls me into his arms, one hand at the small of my back, the other cradling the back of my head like I might drift away again if he lets go.

I rest my cheek against his chest.

His fingers move, drawing slow, lazy circles over my spine. "That was..." He trails off.

I finish it. "Everything."

He huffs a quiet laugh. "Not how I imagined our Infernal Claim."

I smile, eyes still closed. "Same."

"I was going to light candles," he says, teasing. "Maybe play music. Whisper something poetic about your eyes."

I snort. "Oh? What were you thinking—violin and rose petals? Maybe recite a sonnet while you undress me?"

"Something classy," he says, utterly deadpan. "Pachelbel's Canon. Or Marvin Gaye."

I groan into his chest. "Please tell me you're not that guy."

He shrugs, smug. "I contain multitudes."

"You contain delusion."

"Excuse you." He tilts his head, mock-offended. "I had a whole speech planned. There were metaphors. A solid moon comparison."

"What, like your eyes are like twin celestial bodies orbiting my soul?"

He blinks. "...Yes, actually."

I laugh. "Thank god we skipped the poetry. You would've ruined the mood."

"I have something for you," he says suddenly.

He rolls over to the bedside table next to him and pulls something out of the drawer. He has a black velvet box in his hand. *Holy shit is that what I think it is?*

A gasp escapes my lips when he flips open the lid.

The garnet glows like a slow ember—dark red, almost black, like it was pulled from the heart of something deep in Hell. Clawed prongs grip it tight, blackened and raw, like they forged themselves around the stone instead of being set.

The band's not smooth. It's textured with fire and branding.

My throat tightens. It's not just beautiful. It's me.

"I had it made the day your divorce finalized," he says.

My breath catches.

"I didn't say anything. I didn't want it to feel like a prize. Or some finish line I was waiting for you to cross." He swallows. "I just wanted you to know I saw you. That I *see* you."

My fingers brush the edge of the garnet, still trembling. "Why didn't you tell me?"

He shrugs—just a little. "You needed time to choose yourself first. I wanted to be ready the moment you realized you didn't have to be alone anymore."

"You know," I say, voice rough with something I don't want to name, "you could've made this a lot more dramatic."

He smiles, slow. "You've had enough drama."

I huff out a laugh. "So, is this the calm after the storm?"

"No," he says, reaching for my hand, fingers brushing the inside of my wrist. "This is the part where you finally let yourself rest. None of the clean up required after a storm."

I study the ring again, how it looks like it was dragged through fire and hand made with love.

"I didn't think I'd ever do this again," I admit. "Marriage. Rings. Vows."

"Belladonna, I want to marry you."

My breath catches.

"I want to wake up next to you when we're hundreds of years old and still arguing about where to put the mugs. I want to watch you conquer the world, and I want to be there to rub your back when you're tired of carrying it. I want something strong and so damn real it doesn't need prophecy or magic to make it last."

He swallows and turns his body fully towards me. "I love you. I want to love you every ordinary day we're given."

My throat burns.

He holds out the ring again—like a vow, like a life. "Will you marry me?"

"Yes," I shout. "Yes. I will marry you."

He lets out a sound that's half laugh, half disbelieving breath, and then he's kissing me again, both of us grinning like idiots between kisses. It's messy and perfect and nothing hurts.

A small, glowing rift opens near the ceiling with a sound like someone ripping through wet paper and sighing about it.

A scroll drops from it and hits Owen in the shoulder, landing between us.

We both stare at it.

"Should we be worried?" He raises an eyebrow.

I lean over and unroll it. It's written in Ophelia's handwriting. Slightly singed at the edges.

If you two are done making up and/or bonding through hellfire, we're having a family BBQ at the house.

There will be potato salad.

You're bringing dessert. No excuses.

Love you. Mostly.

Your sister

I blink. "Did we just get summoned by scroll?"

"With dessert duty." Owen grins.

I toss it onto the bed and groan. "We just got engaged."

"Exactly," he says, already pulling me up by the hand. "Perfect timing. Let's go show off the ring."

"Can't I have, like, an hour to bask in the moment?"

He's already tugging a shirt over his head. "You can bask while we walk through the murder garden."

"Not without dessert, we can't," I mutter, summoning flame to my palm.

Owen pauses, half-laced boot in his hand. "Please tell me you're not going to burn the cookies again."

I flick my wrist, and a silver platter appears on the nightstand, stacked high with perfectly glazed blood-orange tarts, drizzled in dark honey and garnished with candied rose petals that shimmer faintly with magic.

"This time I just conjured them," I say while I finish getting dressed.

He offers his arm. "After you, fiancée."

I take it, ring glinting. "Let's make an entrance."

But just before we step through the portal, something catches in my chest.

Deja vu.

The last time I walked into one of Ophelia's parties, I was introduced as someone's wife.

Rhys's wife.

My hand tightens slightly around Owen's arm. He feels it. I see it in the way he looks at me. Like I'm his entire world. He is mine. No one else matters at this moment but us.

The murder garden portal blooms wide, spilling gold light and the hum of voices into our bedroom. The scent of jasmine and charred meat rolls through.

When we step through, their conversation halt abruptly, collectively, their heads turn to face us. Ophelia stands near the center, one hand wrapped around a wine glass, mid-sentence—and then she sees the ring on my finger.

"Bella—" she starts.

I lift my hand high, letting the garnet catch the sun. "We're engaged!"

The garden goes dead quiet for three whole seconds. Then the place erupts.

There's cheering. Shouting. Someone pops a bottle of something sparkling and sprays it directly into the air. Two of Owen's cousins rush forward, nearly knocking me over in a hug that smells like smoke and sugar. Ophelia's eyes go glassy before she shoves a plate of potato salad into Julian's hands.

I'm laughing before I even realize it—real, unguarded laughter that bubbles up from somewhere deep.

Because no one here is calculating, or measuring, or trying to stake a claim.

They're just... happy. For us.

Owen squeezes my hand, leaning in so only I hear him. "Told you they'd love it."

I don't even get the chance to reply before Ophelia appears out of nowhere with a noise somewhere between a gasp and a battle cry.

"You're *engaged*?" she squeals, grabbing my left hand and yanking it into the firelight like she's inspecting a priceless artifact. "Oh, that ring is so you. Wait—don't tell me, let me scream first!"

I have to cover my ears from Ophelia's assault on them.

Before I can catch my breath, Selene and Liora swoop in behind her, effectively cutting me off from Owen and dragging me deeper into the garden.

Liora's eyes are already glassy, her smile so wide I'm half-convinced it might split her face. "Another one of my sons is getting married," she says, her voice warm and fierce. "And *mated*. Oh, Bella, this is perfect. First Julian, and now Owen... my heart can hardly take it."

"I just said yes like five minutes ago—" I start.

Ophelia's still squealing, bouncing on her toes. "Do you know what this means? Wedding planning. Dress shopping. Oh, gods, the *menu*."

Selene smirks knowingly. "The Infernal Union."

Liora clasps her hands together, eyes sparkling. "Yes. The Infernal Union. The real ceremony. It will be tradition, spectacle, and magic worthy of the bond you've forged. Oh, the banners will be magnificent."

"We have to start planning!" Ophelia squeals. She pulls me toward the nearest table like the decisions have to be made *right now*.

Selene falls in on my left, already pulling a notebook out of... somewhere. "Colors. We'll start with colors."

"Deep red," Liora says instantly. "Nothing else will do for an Infernal Union." She's glowing, absolutely glowing, her hands clasped like she's holding the whole moment to her chest.

Ophelia slams a chair out for me with her foot and pushes me into it. "We need flowers, music, a menu—no, three menus. Do we want it in the garden or the grand hall? The garden has better light, the hall has better acoustics for the vows and both can handle the explosion of fire."

"I...um...I—" I stammer.

Liora leans forward, eyes alight. "We *must* have the bloodmoon for the ceremony."

I glance over my shoulder to find Owen watching from across the lawn, hands in his pockets, looking infuriatingly entertained as his family hijacks my engagement.

"I just got engaged," I protest weakly.

"And now you're getting married," Ophelia says, already sketching what I think might be a dress design on Selene's notepad. "You're welcome."

I lean back in my chair, pretending to study the scribbles. "Okay this is a lot. It's just a wedding!"

Three sets of eyes turn to me at once.

Ophelia's grin goes feral. Selene tips her head, studying me like she's weighing how much truth I can handle. And Liora just... smiles.

"Oh, Bella. It's so much more than that," Liora says, her voice wavering from laughter. "You'll find out soon enough."

Chapter Twenty
Owen

This was not what I was expecting when I got summoned to a loft in the city. The man has been pacing for a solid two minutes straight at this point, not saying anything at all.

I'm more trapped here watching him than I've ever been with those stupid demon 'traps' others have set. "Why did you summon me?" I ask, breaking the silence.

"I just followed the steps and called someone," the man says, breathless. "I guess that's you."

He walks up to me, eyes wild and needy. "I want to make a deal," he says.

"That's rather obvious, don't you think?" I say. "Go on, then, I'm listening."

"My girlfriend broke up with me," he blurts. He starts pacing again, raking his hand through his hair. "I've been waiting forever to be with her and she just left. I want her back."

I tilt my head. "And what exactly do you want from me?"

He stops, turning toward me like the words cost him something. "I want her to want me again. Want me in her bed. Like before."

Pathetic. Yet... those are the easiest.

"You're asking me to alter her mind," I say, more a statement than a question.

His gaze flickers, but he holds it. "She loves me. She just—forgot. I just need her to remember. To want me."

"Mm." I circle him slowly. He smells like sawdust and desperation. "What if she remembers, and still leaves?"

"She won't."

There it is—that human certainty, blind as a newborn, convinced the future bends to their desires.

I stop in front of him. "I can give you a window. She'll think of you, crave you, ache for you. Long enough for you to believe it's real. But when the hunger fades, she'll see you exactly as you are."

He swallows, hard. "That's fine."

"Is it?" I let the question hang between us. "Because if you aren't enough, you'll lose her all over again. And I'll still have my payment."

"What is it?"

"You'll know when I take it." My smirk is predatory.

He nods too fast, like a drowning man grabbing a rope without checking where it leads.

I smile. "We have a deal."

A flick of my wrist and the contract manifests—black parchment edged with faint gold light, the letters of his name already faintly etched into the surface, waiting.

I draw a slim silver blade across his palm. "Press it here."

He flinches, but obeys. Blood runs hot over his skin, filling the lines of his palm. When he presses his hand to the parchment, the gold outline flares red. The blood sinks into the page, the shape now sharp and permanent. His wound seals instantly, but the stain of the act will never wash from him.

Jasper Wilder. Bound.

I portal back to Hell before the glow fades.

The Accord's main hall has brass tubes lining endless black shelves, ledgers stacked like bricks, the scent of parchment and scorched iron hanging in the air.

At the obsidian counter, Selene looks up. Her curly, auburn hair swings over one shoulder, eyes brightening when she sees me.

"Well, if it isn't my favorite nephew," she says, setting her quill down. "You bring me something good, or is this another one of your I-swear-it's-interesting contracts?"

I slide the parchment toward her. "You'll see."

She glances at the bloody handprint, brows lifting. "Ooh. Messy. I like it." She dips her quill. "Name?"

"Jasper Wilder."

"Nature of the request?" She mutters, jotting it down.

"Rekindle romantic and physical desire in his ex-girlfriend. Whoever she is."

Selene smirks. "Oh, so just a little thing. No big deal. Totally worth eternal consequences." She stamps the parchment in deep red wax, the iron tang filling the air, and slides it into a brass tube. It clicks shut with a satisfying finality.

"Filed. Awaiting activation," she says, then adds with a grin, "Tell him to send a thank you card when it all blows up in his face."

I shake my head. "You're terrible."

"I'm honest," she says, already reaching for the next file. "Go on, nephew. You've got an Infernal Union to plan."

"I do?" I ask, raising a brow.

"Not yet, but soon," she chuckles out.

I leave and still hear her laughing in the distance.

It'll still be a while before Bella gets home from Hearthlight, they're busy today.

I've been checking in on her sporadically, I'm worried about her. This is her first day back to work. After everything that's happened, normalcy is what she needs.

Kind of normal. With my ring on her finger, she's bound to stand out.

I am deciding what to do when I hear her voice. Strong and clear.

Arabella: *Do you have a second?*

Owen: *Anything for you. What's up?*

Arabella: *Well...*

Owen: *What's wrong?*

Arabella: *Rhys is here.*

I don't respond, instead I portal straight into her office. This fucker. He just doesn't know when to leave shit alone.

The first thing I see when I get into Bella's office is Rhys. Smug smile and all.

"Of course she called you," he says, voice dripping with disdain.

"My mate doesn't like to deal with gnats that won't leave her alone."

"Careful," Rhys says, leaning back against the wall. "You might make me think you matter."

I cross the room, drop an arm around Bella, pulling her close to my side like I don't even hear him. She's shaking. "What do you need?"

Rhys's smile falters, just a fraction. He hates being ignored more than he hates me—which is saying something.

Bella's gaze flicks between us. "I don't know why he's here, Owen. I just know it's not good."

"You have two seconds to tell us why you came," I say, looking at Rhys.

"Now why would I do that?" Rhys says, smirking at me before turning his attention to his nails like I'm not worth his time. "Instead, I can wait for the fun to begin."

He sees it. The ring.

His smirk freezes for a fraction of a second. "Well, well... not even a year. Guess you didn't waste any time finding someone else to keep your bed warm."

"What the hell are you doing in my office, Rhys?" Bella asks. She's clearly out of patience.

"Just thought I'd drop in. See who's been keeping you busy." His eyes flick to the ring again, more irritated this time. "Looks like they've been *very* busy."

"Cut the shit," she snaps. "You didn't come here to catch up."

"No," he says, giving me a smile that marks the worst humanity can offer, "I came to see if you were still making the same mistakes. But you... you're moving on so fast you'll probably lap yourself."

Her voice goes icy. "The only mistake here is letting you stand in my office for more than thirty seconds. Get the fuck out before I make you regret it."

"I'm not done just yet, sweetheart." For just a moment, his jaw tightens — the tell. The mask slides back on.

"Get to it, Westwood," I growl.

"Oh, is the little demon scared?" He chuckles.

I can feel Bella tense next to me. She's one more word from losing it completely.

"You'll find out in about 30 seconds," he says. We both hear a ding on her computer. "It's time."

I see she has an email from Tinsley.

From: Tinsley Creed <t.creed@hearthlight.org>

To: Arabella Arden <a.arden@hearthlight.org>

Subject: Don't panic. I'm on it.

Bella,

Before you hear about it from someone else, I want you to see it straight from me.

The North Star Journal — Your Compass for the Truth

Published by Creed Media Group

The Dangerous Heart of Hearthlight: When Empathy Enables Evil

Yes, it's Westwood. Yes, it's ugly. I've already looped Julia in — she's combing through it for anything legally actionable. In the meantime, I'm drafting our public response and flagging friendly reporters for interviews so we get our side out first.

You keep doing the work that matters—I'll make sure this garbage doesn't stick.

—Tinsley

"Are you fucking kidding me?" Bella's voice ricochets through the office.

Rhys looks up from where he's leaning on her desk, his smug grin freezing as she barrels toward him.

"You hate me, I get that," she snaps. "Fine. But to put all of these women in danger just so you can get back at me?" She jabs a finger toward his chest. "That's the reason I divorced you. You've always been selfish, Rhys—but this?"

He starts to speak, but she steamrolls over him, eyes blazing. "I got lucky with Owen. I was a dipshit to ever marry you."

His jaw ticks. That's the hit. That's the one he can't let go unanswered. "Right," he says slowly. "You got *lucky* with Owen. Guess he doesn't mind that you've been passed around more than a damn bottle at a frat party."

My stomach knots, but he isn't done. "Hell, maybe that's what keeps him interested. New tricks for an old toy."

I step in before she has to answer. "Careful, Westwood. I'm not in the mood to pretend you're worth letting live."

For half a second, he blinks—like he wasn't expecting me to bite back—but the smug mask snaps right back in place.

Bella shakes her head and goes back to her computer. She clicks on the link the article pops up. I read along with her over her shoulder.

The North Star Journal

Your Compass for the Truth

Published by Creed Media Group

The Dangerous Heart of Hearthlight: When Empathy Enables Evil

By Rhys Westwood | Senior Investigative Contributor

"You want to believe she's doing good," says a former staff member who spoke on the condition of anonymity. "But at Hearthlight, good intentions don't protect anyone. They hide the danger."

For years, Arabella Arden's nonprofit Hearthlight has been celebrated as a beacon of compassion—a sanctuary for the vulnerable, the lost, and those "no one else will take in."

But a *North Star Journal* investigation—drawing on interviews with former staff, leaked internal communications, and a troubling review of past incidents—suggests the organization's heart may be dangerously unshielded...and its leader dangerously unstable.

A Pattern of Reckless Decision Making

In at least three separate cases over the past eighteen months, residents with violent criminal histories were reportedly granted full access to Hearthlight's common areas without security oversight.

A former security contractor told *The North Star Journal*, *"We weren't given full background checks on new intakes. More than once, I found out about violent pasts after incidents happened—and when I brought it up, I was told to 'trust Arabella's judgment.'"*

The Unregulated Haven

Unlike licensed care facilities, Hearthlight is not subject to the same licensing requirements—a loophole Arden has allegedly exploited to operate with no external oversight. According to public records reviewed by *The North Star Journal*, the nonprofit has faced no state inspections since its founding.

"She treats it like her personal kingdom," says another former staffer. "If she likes you, you get special treatment. If she doesn't, you're gone."

Leaked Emails Raise Questions

Internal emails obtained by *The North Star Journal* appear to show Arden overruling staff concerns in at least two high risk situations. In one, when warned that a new resident had a restraining order filed against them, Arden replied: *"We don't judge people by paper. Everyone here gets a clean slate."*

Days later, that resident was involved in a physical altercation that sent another to the hospital.

Personal Tragedy: "She Took Everything From Me"

In perhaps the most emotional account, one former resident claims Hearthlight directly led to the loss of her family.

Tiana Holloway, who stayed at Hearthlight, alleges that after what she describes as a "private disagreement" with her husband, Arabella Arden called the police—resulting in his arrest.

"It was a personal matter. We just needed space to work things out," Holloway says, her voice breaking. *"Instead, she turned it into a crime*

scene. They took him away in handcuffs. I haven't seen him since. And she called child services when she didn't have to. My kids were gone. I'll never get them back. She destroyed my family."

Public records confirm that Holloway's husband was arrested during her stay at Hearthlight and later disappeared. Her children were removed from her custody shortly afterward. The details of both cases remain sealed.

Blurred Boundaries

Multiple sources allege Arden frequently becomes personally involved with residents' disputes, sometimes escalating tensions rather than diffusing them.

One ex-volunteer claims, *"She takes everything personally. If she's having a good day, maybe she'll listen. If not, she'll throw you out in front of everyone."*

The Public Image vs. the Reality□

On social media, Arden is a tireless advocate, posting smiling photos with residents and staff. But several former employees claim those moments were staged.

"She'd be screaming at someone one minute and posting an inspirational quote the next," says one.

I look at the evidence he claims to have. A redacted email with the "clean slate" section. A report detailing over 100 covered incidents in the last year. Most of them redacted, except for Tiana's.

It looks like he's implying a cover up.

Closing Paragraph

Advocates for nonprofit oversight argue that organizations like Hearthlight must meet minimum safety standards and undergo regular inspections.

"Compassion is important," says Marla Trent, director of the Safe Havens Coalition, "but compassion without safeguards puts people at risk."

Hearthlight may present itself as a beacon in the dark—but when the light is left unguarded, it doesn't guide the lost. It kills it.

Bella's hands are shaking so hard she almost drops her phone. Her eyes are red, wet, and glassy, but it's not just crying—it's that look someone gets when their whole life has just been yanked out from under them.

It's bad. Career ending bad. He didn't just take a shot at her—he fired a fucking missile. And he may have hit his target.

She turns to me, completely ignoring Rhys. Her breath comes fast, uneven. "He—he's trying to end me, Owen."

"He's trying," I say. "That doesn't mean he'll succeed."

She shakes her head, tears streaking down her cheeks. "No, you don't understand. This—this is the kind of thing you don't come back from. Sponsors, donors...the parents I work with—" Her voice breaks and she presses her fists against her mouth.

I roll her chair back so she can look at me. "Let Tinsley and Julia handle it."

"Owen—"

"No." I tip her chin up so she's forced to meet my eyes. "Look at me. I've spent my entire life dealing with men like him. He's counting on you to fold. To panic. To drown yourself in this until you forget you can swim. You're not giving him that."

Her eyes search mine, desperate, like she's trying to believe me but the ground's still falling away beneath her.

That is until another ding changes our lives. I look at the email from Tinsley. It's just a link, but it's hope. Rhys must have received one too considering all of the color drained from his face.

Hearthlight Official Statement

Issued by Tinsley Creed, Director of Communications

This morning, *The North Star Journal*, a Creed Media Group publication, ran an article by Rhys Westwood targeting our founder, Arabella Arden. We are responding in full because the public deserves the truth.

1. Conflict of Interest

Mr. Westwood is Ms. Arden's ex-husband. They divorced less than a year ago, and Ms. Arden is now engaged. This is a critical fact he failed to disclose in his "investigation." Readers are entitled to know when a reporter's work is fueled by personal bitterness rather than journalistic integrity.

2. The Tiana Holloway Claims

Ms. Holloway alleges Ms. Arden "destroyed" her family. Here is what she left out:

- On the night in question, Ms. Holloway's husband arrived at Hearthlight uninvited, threatened staff, and threatened Ms. Arden directly.

- Staff followed state law by calling police. Mr. Holloway was arrested for multiple counts of harassment and assault.

- Child Protective Services became involved automatically due to the incident, as required by law—not at Ms. Arden's personal request.

- The decision to remove the children was made by CPS, not Hearthlight.

- Public records show Ms. Holloway had prior CPS involvement before ever arriving at Hearthlight.

This is not opinion—it is a documented fact.

3. Anonymous "Sources"

Every unnamed source in this article has either:

- Been removed from Hearthlight for misconduct,

- Lost civil cases against the organization, or

- Has direct financial ties to Creed Media Group.

The most quoted "security contractor" was terminated for violent behavior toward a resident. The "former volunteer" who claimed Ms. Arden "throws people out" was caught stealing from the center's donation funds.

4. The Real Motive

For over two years, Creed Media Group has attempted to purchase Hearthlight's property. Ms. Arden has refused every offer.

The sudden publication of this article—riddled with omissions, distortions, and outright falsehoods—came less than three weeks after the most recent failed acquisition attempt. The connection is not a coincidence.

5. To Rhys Westwood

Your attempt to destroy Ms. Arden's work says far more about you than it does about her. The personal malice behind this piece is evident to anyone who reads it. You did not write to protect anyone—you wrote to punish someone who moved on without you.

We will not allow this smear to go unanswered. Our legal counsel, Julia Carter, is already reviewing the article for defamation, ethical violations, and potential malicious interference with a nonprofit organization.

To our community: We stand on our record. We stand by our founder. And we stand by every person who has found safety here, no matter how many lies are printed to take that away.

Tinsley Creed

Director of Communications, Hearthlight

I hear Bella's boisterous laugh as she reads this. It also helps that Tinsley opened up the page for comments.

Tinsley's statement has been up for less than an hour and it's already pushing sixty thousand shares. Her words gutted Rhys Westwood in broad daylight—and now the internet's piling on with torches and gasoline.

@SophieTruth

So let me get this straight—Rhys Westwood is Bella's ex-husband, didn't disclose it, and wrote a hit piece right after she got engaged. My friend worked at Hearthlight. That "security contractor" he quoted? Fired for shoving a resident into a wall. This article is trash.

@RavenReceipts

Ohhh so this is about property. Creed Media wants the land. Always follow the money. Also, his "sources" are all people fired from Hearthlight—Rhys just group-texted the bitter ex-employee's club.

@BookishBitterMuch

"Moved on without you"—chef's kiss. Tinsley just ended that man's career and wrote his obituary in one press release. Imagine losing your wife, losing the building you wanted, and losing your dignity in 1,500 words. Couldn't be me.

@FirebrandFiles

Tiana Holloway? I used to work with her. She had CPS on her YEARS before Hearthlight. This is all lies. Bella is out here changing lives while Rhys plays keyboard warrior from his sad little Creed Media desk.

@LexHotTea

Rhys "Unbiased Journalist" Westwood forgot to mention he's Bella's ex. Bro wrote a diary entry, not an article. "Dangerous Heart of Hearthlight" sounds like bad poetry he wrote drunk and crying.

@UrbanDumpster

So Rhys lost his wife, lost the building he wanted, and now he's gonna lose his job. When your ex won't text you back so you write a 2,000-word smear campaign—peak masculinity.

@SpillTheLaw

If you Google "journalistic ethics," Rhys Westwood's face is the before picture. Julia Carter's about to make him wish he'd stuck to Yelp reviews.

@HearthlightStrong

We love you, Bella. You've changed lives. No headline can take that away.

The likes are racking up in real time. The more she scrolls, the clearer it is—Rhys thought he was ending her career, but Tinsley flipped it so hard the man's social life won't survive the week.

Bella looks up from the screen. Rhys is still scrolling, his jaw tight, face pale. "This is what accountability looks like, you bastard."

He freezes, eyes flicking to hers. For once, there's no snide remark or smug comeback.

When he finally moves, it's only to glare at her like he could burn a hole straight through her. He turns on his heel and slams the door hard enough to rattle the glass.

I pull Bella into my arms, feeling the tremor still running through her. "Now what?"

She sighs before looking up at me with a spark in her eyes that wasn't there before. "We get married."

Chapter Twenty-One

Arabella

I t's my wedding day. I married Rhys in a courthouse. It wasn't personal or romantic. This couldn't be more different.

The Infernal Union is a private, family-only event. As much as I would love my friends to be here, they couldn't. Demons and mates only. Especially since the Infernal Council signs off on it. They're terrifying to mortals.

There's not a hint of apprehension or uncertainty in my heart. Every single part of me wants to be with Owen for the rest of our lives, our incredibly long lives.

"Are you ready for hair and makeup?" Ophelia asks.

"Yes!" I'm almost bouncing like a school girl going to her first prom. I know for a fact that my chest and face are flushed.

She smiles, almost as giddy as me, goes to the door and waves her hand. Two women come in, arms weighed down with bags.

"Hi, Bella," one says. She's all smooth lines and quiet confidence—dark, glossy hair twisted into a sleek knot, warm brown skin that seems to catch the light, and eyes the color of molten amber. Even carrying half a salon in her hands, she looks like she could step onto a runway without missing a beat. "My name is Gianna Ellery."

"Ellery?" I ask, furrowing my brows. "Are you related to Raymond Ellery?"

"I'm his soulmate," she lilts, the words sliding out like silk.

They go straight to work. Gianna and her assistant focus on my hair first—it's still damp from my shower. They blow dry it, then set it in huge rollers.

While that sets, they start on my makeup. Gianna keeps my skin fresh and dewy, adds a sharp statement eyeliner, and paints my lips a deep crimson.

When the rollers come out, my hair's full of volume with soft curls. It's perfect.

Gianna gives me a final once over before she steps back with a satisfied smile. "She's ready."

I turn around and see Ophelia. She moves in immediately, hands light but purposeful. "Alright, let's get you into your dress."

The dress is deep crimson silk, cut in a way that skims my body without clinging. The high neckline is simple and strong, drawing the eye upward, while the back... the back is nothing but skin and two thin silk straps crossing low between my shoulder blades.

The skirt falls smooth and straight to the floor, but the silk shifts and flows with every movement, like smoke curling in slow motion.

Ophelia helps me step into the dress, careful not to snag the silk. "You look beautiful."

I can feel the tears forming in my eyes.

"I'm glad I have you," I say.

Her hands pause on the fabric. She looks up at me, and her voice wavers just a little. "I don't know who I'd be without you."

That's it. The dam breaks. "You've always been there," I whisper, my voice shaking. "Every good thing, every bad thing—you were the one who never left. You were always my rock."

Her eyes shine, but she's smiling through it. "We've been through hell together. And somehow... we still laugh. We still find each other."

I nod, blinking hard. "You're my home, Ophelia."

She pulls me into her arms, holding on like she's never letting go. "And you're mine," she murmurs. "No matter what changes, that never will."

We stand there, clinging to each other, both of us crying—because this is the truth of us. Before the ceremony, before the titles and the vows, before everything else... we were sisters. We always will be.

"Enough with the tears," Ophelia says, backing up. "Your fated mate is waiting for you."

This ceremony is the cherry on top. It finalizes our bond in an incredibly meaningful way. At least, that's what they're all telling me.

I slip my shoes on slowly—deep red satin heels, the exact shade of my bouquet. The straps cross delicately over my ankles, cool against my skin, and the moment they're buckled, I feel... complete. Like the last piece has clicked into place.

The silk of my dress whispers with every shift, pooling at my feet as I stand.

We're having the ceremony in one of the oldest chambers in Hell—a vaulted space carved into black marble, with firelight dancing along the walls. It feels sacred, ancient, as if it's been waiting for this day long before I ever existed.

Ophelia hands me my bouquet. The deep crimson blooms look like they've been painted in shadow, the petals so soft they almost melt under my fingers.

We step into the corridor together, the sound of our footsteps swallowed by the heavy hush of the space. Torches line the walls, their flames bending as we pass, as if bowing in silent acknowledgment. Somewhere ahead, faint music drifts through the air, like a heartbeat pulling me forward.

The passage curves before the chamber opens before us—vast, vaulted, carved in black marble that gleams in the firelight.

This is where it will happen. Where we will stand. Where we will be bound in yet another way.

Ophelia squeezes my hand once, her thumb brushing over my knuckles, and then she lets go. I can feel her pride and her love like a hug I'll carry to the altar.

The double doors swing open.

For a heartbeat, I can't move—can't breathe. Tall braziers line the aisle, their flames stretching upward, shadows dancing across the walls. The air smells faintly of smoke and something older, something sacred.

And there, at the far end, is Owen.

The closer I get, the louder my heart pounds. It's not nerves. It's the gravity of this moment, the way it feels carved into the fabric of everything I am.

By the time I reach him, it's like the rest of the room has fallen away. Just him and me. And the promise we're about to seal.

The Infernal Council looms above us, seated on a towering black stone dais. Their cloaked figures blur in the firelight, eyes—or something like eyes—glinting faintly from the shadows. Two columns of living flame rise on either side of us, curling high toward the vaulted ceiling. The heat is searing, a predator circling too close.

We step forward together. The flames hiss, parting just enough to let us pass, their heat clawing at our skin.

The Circle of Witnesses closes in—family, allies, and enemies alike, each one armed. Some stand to guard us. Some to test us.

At the center waits the brazier and even more fire, thick with the scent of oil and iron. Owen goes first—cutting his palm so the blood runs hot and red into the flames. He offers his weapon, a blade older than the mortal realm, and speaks his full name.

I follow. My blood hisses in the fire. I offer my dagger, its curve wicked and familiar, and give my name.

The flames roar higher. The Council leans forward. Their voices join into one—low, resonant, inescapable.

"Do you stand here as one who will never call the other a weakness?"

I lift my chin. "I do. He is not my weakness."

Owen's voice is steel. "She is my edge."

"If the world falls, what will you do?"

"I will fall beside him," I answer without pause.

"If war comes to your gates, what will you be to each other?"

"You are my shield," I say.

"I am your blade," he replies, his eyes locked on mine like there's no one else here.

"Do you choose this bond freely?"

"I chose this," I say.

"I choose you still," Owen answers.

The Council watches for a long, charged moment. Then the brazier erupts, a column of black gold flame wrapping around us, burning so hot I swear it sears my bones. My Mark ignites, reshaping under my skin, a crown of flame encircling it. Owen's glows the same.

We are led to the Throne of Ash and seated side by side. The Council rises as one, their cloaks shifting like a single dark wave.

The bond is recognized. The union is sealed. In that moment, we are not just two souls tied together—we are dominions, bound and dangerous, untouchable to anyone but each other.

Everyone is cheering and clapping for us, but it's all just noise compared to the way Owen's looking at me. Like the rest of the room doesn't exist.

He leans in, his hand cupping the side of my face, his thumb brushing over my cheek. The kiss is slow at first before it deepens, and the cheers fade until there's only the heat of his mouth on mine.

"Let's party!" Ophelia exclaims.

We all head back to our house. Everything is set up and waiting for us.

There are black petals scattered all over the living room floor. Low tables are arranged in a wide circle, covered in deep crimson table cloths, heavy silver goblets, and bowls of food spread across the room.

Candles float in shallow vases of dark water. The house smells like honey wine and spiced meat. Music hums in the background.

"You went all out," I say, turning to Ophelia.

"I didn't do it." She lifts her chin towards Owen.

My gaze swings back to him. "You did all of this?"

"Only the best for my soulmate," he says, kissing me again.

"You didn't have to," I murmur.

"Yeah," he says softly, brushing his thumb over my cheek. "I did."

I glance down at his hand where it rests against my face, catching the gleam of the wedding band now sitting beside his ring finger. A thick band of blackened metal with a thin line of gold running through it, like fire trapped inside. It's not delicate or not subtle. It's him.

"Do you like it?" I ask.

His brows lift. "Of course I do. You think I'm the kind of man who would wear something that he does not like?" He catches my left hand, turning it so my own ring catches the light. "The whole realm will know how much I love it. That's the point of wearing one."

I shake my head, a small laugh slipping out. "You're such a hopeless romantic."

"Maybe," he says, leaning closer, "but I'm yours."

We're pulled into the center of the gathering where we receive more toasts, more congratulations, more laughter. Owen never leaves my side. Even when he's speaking to someone else, his hand stays at my back, a constant. When we finally slip away, it's like the night itself makes room for us.

In the courtyard outside our bedroom, the garden stretches out, still lit by lanterns and firelight. I can hear our friends talking, laughing, the sound softened by distance. Owen steps up behind me, his arms sliding around my waist, his chin resting lightly on my shoulder.

"Married," he murmurs.

I turn in his arms, pressing my hands to his chest. "Married."

For a moment we just look at each other. He tilts his head, brushing his mouth over mine in a kiss that's slow and certain, like we have all the time in the world, which I suppose we do. When we finally break apart, his forehead rests against mine.

"I love you," I say.

His smile is almost wicked. "Good. You're stuck with me now."

I laugh, and he kisses me again, the lantern light catching on both our rings—twin flashes of gold in the dark.

My life has been a series of bad choices. Promises. False forever. But this time...this time, with him, forever doesn't feel like it's long enough.

Epilogue
Lucas

I'm getting a call. Owen, of course. Apparently Bella's friend, Josie Brighton, is moving into her boyfriend's place.

She needs help packing since he's busy. Seems like she's the one doing all the heavy lifting while he keeps trying to claim he has to work.

Naturally, my sisters-in-law decided this is a perfect excuse for a packing party. I'm not surprised—they'd throw a party for anything.

Even less shocking? All the Duvains got roped into it. Not that I mind because I love Bella and Lia. I just don't want to spend my night off packing boxes.

Still, I can't be the only one who doesn't show. So, I shower first. No point walking in covered in soul... goop. We've never really given it a name.

By the time I make it to Bella's old apartment, the place is crawling with Duvains. Owen's by the door, sleeves rolled up, barking orders like he's leading a war council.

Julian and Seth were wrestling a dresser through the hallway, nearly taking the doorframe with it. Damian was in the kitchen, pulling open cabinets and muttering about expired cereal. Adrian was halfway out the window for some reason, and Caleb had a box under one arm while scrolling through his phone with the other.

"We portal ourselves," Damian grunted, "but we move our stuff."

"What is this, the dark ages?" Adrian called from the window.

It was a *packing party*, apparently, because she was moving into a mortal's place — and apparently that meant doing things the mortal way.

I step inside and lean against the wall, watching them for a moment.

"Look who finally decided to show," Seth calls, grinning. "About time, Sloth."

"Yeah," Julian adds, not looking up from a box of dishes. "Did you have to stop and take a nap on the way here?"

"Yeah yeah yeah," I say. "All of you shut up."

The voices in the room blur, fading under the sound of footsteps from the hallway. A shadow moves in the doorway first before she steps into the light.

Blonde curls catch against her sweatshirt, pulled up into a messy knot on top of her head, held with something sparkly. The glitter doesn't belong in this dusty apartment, but it clings to her anyway. Colorful leggings flash against the dull beige walls, her sneakers soft against the floor. She carries a box that should slow her down, but she moves quick, easy—like she's spent her life carrying things for everyone else.

Her eyes lift, scanning the room. Then they find me.

Something flares on my left forearm. I glance down, and a mark is blooming there, curling into my skin like it's burning its way in.

Across the room, she gasps. The box slips from her hands, hitting the floor with a hollow thud.

She starts screaming.

The sound rips through the apartment, raw enough to freeze every Duvain mid motion. Her knees buckle, and she crumples to the floor, hands clutching at her chest like she's trying to hold something in—or keep something out.

The mark on my arm burns hotter, flaring like it knows she's here. My chest tightens. And then I'm moving—fast—pushing past boxes and bodies, zeroed in on her like there's no one else in the room.

Bella and Ophelia are the first to move. They're at her side in seconds, kneeling on the worn carpet. Ophelia's voice is trying to ground her. Bella's hands are pushing Josie's hair back, murmuring something I can't hear.

"You're marked," Bella says, her voice tight.

Josie shakes her head, gasping. "No—no, it hurts. Is my baby okay?"

The word sticks. *Baby?*

I step forward before I can stop myself. "Baby?"

Her eyes lock on mine—green, wet, terrified. "I'm pregnant," she says.

The mark on my arm sears white hot once again. And everything else goes silent.

Up Next

Up Next in The Devil's Bargain Series...

(Book Three – Sloth)

He's never been in a hurry for anything.

She's spent her whole life giving too much, too fast.

But Sloth isn't just about waiting.

It's about taking your time to destroy something beautiful.

Coming March 2026

Can't wait? More Devil's Bargain stories are coming for you soon.

Wicked Union

You met them in The Devil's Canvas. Liora and Evander's story coming soon...

October 1, 2025

Preorder Here: https://a.co/d/8MBjBlE

Unholy Vows

You met them in The Devil's Canvas. Selene & Theron's story is
coming soon...
December 1, 2025
Preorder Here: https://a.co/d/a0FxaI7

Extended Epilogue

You've seen the ending. Now see it through Josie's eyes—the way she felt, the things she didn't say, and the moment that changed everything.

Sign up for my newsletter to get the exclusive Josie POV epilogue free: https://BookHip.com/LNGCXMG

Bonus

Don't Leave Without Your Bonus!

Love *Gilded Lies*? You'll want to grab your free digital extras! Your stickers and Bookmarks are just a download away!

Download your set here: https://drive.google.com/drive/folders/1OvrJ-HcFk-2RCJCttMOyrtAR1b0-U2K3?usp=sharing

About the Author

Deliciously Dark, Beautifully Twisted

Sara McClaflin writes dark romance with feelings, flaws, and just the right amount of emotional damage. Her stories are character-driven, morally gray, and often ask one very important question: what if love was a little dangerous—and we liked it that way? After years of reading and reviewing books with too much angst, she finally started writing her own.

She lives on the West Coast with her husband, their chaotic dog, and more book boyfriends than she's willing to admit. Her TBR pile is a cry for help, her playlists are 80% heartbreak, and she's always chasing the next character who'll ruin her in the best way.

Newsletter Sign up: https://subscribepage.io/saras-newsletter

amazon.com/stores/Sara-McClaflin/author/B0CR8VHBHJ?ref=ap_rdr&isDramIntegrated=true&shoppingPortalEnabled=true&ccs_id=1fcaa1c2-62ac-4142-ab01-dce9c490e471

bookbub.com/profile/sara-mcclaflin

goodreads.com/author/show/47632250.Sara_McClaflin

instagram.com/authorsaramcclaflin/

facebook.com/profile.php?id=61551822185090&notif_id=1744228205391402&notif_t=page_user_activity&ref=notif#

tiktok.com/@sara.mcclaflin

Also By

The Devil's Bargain

The Devil's Canvas

Gilded Lies

The Shadow Brides

Veil of Fire

The Huntington Brothers Series

Destined for Love

Tangled Hearts

Promises to Keep

Standalone Novels

The Keeper's Secret

Love on the Edge

Anthologies

Head in the Clouds: A Romantic Comedy Anthology

Desperate: A Deadly Thriller Anthology

Did you love *Gilded Lies*?

If you enjoyed the story, I would be so grateful if you took a moment to leave a quick review. Thank you for reading, for your support, and for spending time with these characters. I can't wait for you to see what happens next!